IT STARTED

WITH A

Swipe

About the Author

Shelly Smith has spent the majority of her 30s searching for Mr Right. When telling people stories of her dating escapades, they'd often say 'you should write this down!'

So she did. Shelly lives in Manchester where she was born and raised, briefly moved to Wales for 8 years, works in radio, spends most of her time eating sweets, then exercising to release the guilt of eating the sweets.

You can find out more about Shelly by following her on social media:
Instagram @itstartedwithaswipe
Facebook @itstartedwithaswipe
Twitter   @swipegirl

Or you can follow her blog at itstartedwithaswipe.com.

IT STARTED

WITH A

Swipe

Shelly Smith

For Sean. Where it all began.

Username:
Shels81

About:
Non-Smoker with athletic body type (this may be a slight lie)

City:
Manchester, UK

Details:
34-year-old Female, 5' 4" (163cm)

Intent:
Shels81 is looking for a relationship

Education:
Bachelors Degree

Personality:
Silly

Profession:
Radio Producer

About Shelly:
I like: sunsets, the sun, the coast, silliness, red wine, biscuits, travelling, yoga, cake, gin, cheese & exercise.
I dislike: whisky, marzipan, Frazzles, cabbage, sprouts, time wasters & weirdos.

First Date:
A glass of red? A coffee? Cake?

Chapter One

As a teen, I was a nightmare.

I fancied EVERY boy in the year below me in school. And the year above me. I used to go to spin the bottle parties and snog every boy possible – which I'm sure if my parents knew, they'd be horrified. When I actually look back, I'm pretty horrified myself.

Let's move on.

I then started drinking alcohol and I'd go out clubbing. My mates and I used to have competitions in nightclubs to see who could snog the most boys (21 was my record, FYI). No wonder I used to get tonsillitis so often.

Again, we should probably move on.

I got a job working in Sainsbury's as a 'checkout chick' when I was 16 and managed to pull James off the bakery on a Christmas party night out. He wanted to be a dentist. I was going to be a rich married woman. His mum collected frogs… so did I! It was meant to be!

He took me to my first (and only) ever Manchester United football match; I used to go and watch him play rugby and we'd go drinking after the matches; he'd cook for me; we'd sit and watch films together; listen to Robbie Williams together. We used to call each other's landlines for hours to talk because mobile phones didn't exist. Imagine that!

On my 17th birthday, my parents invited him over for a 'birthday tea'. When he arrived, he handed me a gift. It was in a round box. My sisters and myself presumed it was a watch! It was definitely in a watch-shaped box. Everyone crowded round me as I opened it… the box said 'Swarovski' on it. Had he bought me a Swarovski crystal watch?

No. No he hadn't.

He'd bought me a crystal dog, telling me 'it was the first of many to come'. It wasn't even a frog! My sisters sniggered off into the kitchen whilst I thanked him for such a wonderful present… just what I'd always wanted. Sadly, James and I didn't last much longer after my birthday. He's now known to my friends as Crystal Dog Boy.

*****

Not long after, I finally managed to bag Simon who was in the same year as me at school. All the girls in school fancied him. Many of them had been out with him. It was my dream.

He had a friend called James who I guess was kinda cute. He had been repeatedly asking me out. So I decided I'd give it a go with the plan being to show Simon how much fun I was so that he'd fall in love with me and I'd have to dump his mate. But it'd be ok, James would understand. He'd probably be the best man at our wedding and talk about how Simon 'stole' me off him…

Anyway, the plan only went and bloody worked! Who knew?!

Simon and I dated for about 18 months. This was it. He was

THE ONE. He was in a band. Singer and guitar player. Only slight problem was his band played FULL ON HEAVY METAL MUSIC and I was a massive Mariah Carey fan so we couldn't be more opposite. It didn't matter. He used to sit on his bed with his guitar and sing me *More Than Words* by Extreme. I LOVED him.

When we got to 18, the time came to go to university. Simon was going to Sheffield, I was going to Bradford. 'Both in Yorkshire, this can work. This WILL work!' I kept telling myself. My aunty and uncle managed it years ago, probably before landline phones existed, so Simon and I could 100 per cent do it too!

We somehow survived our entire first year at university staying together. Getting on trains every weekend. I would be so excited to see him stood waiting at the train station for me. We'd hug and snog like we didn't care if we were over PDA-ing.

By this point we had also both got mobile phones. The most basic mobile phones ever but it was great! We could call each other whenever we wanted! We just had to top them up! I used to call him 17 times a day. It didn't matter if he didn't answer. I just loved hearing his voice on his answer phone. 'Hi, you've reached Simon's phone, I'm probably out drunk having fun, or in a lecture. Leave me a message and I'll call you back.'

Except one day he stopped calling me back.

He'd fallen in love with someone else. SomeTHING else. Vodka and cannabis.

I loved vodka. He loved cannabis. The two didn't seem to mix. I'd go out and get drunk and call him over and over again. He wouldn't answer. I'd call again. And again. This became my life. Getting drunk, calling him, not hearing back from him. Repeatedly. He was too busy getting stoned to remember who I was. By the time the summer came round, he was such a stoner that I could no longer handle it. I braved it and gave him an ultimatum… it was me or the weed. Thankfully (now I look back at it) he chose the weed. But at the time, I was heart broken. I remember I couldn't even eat a bag of Maltesers the night it happened. That's how heart broken I was.

So I spent the summer with a broken heart. Then went back to uni in September single and ready to mingle!

*****

Sadly, I enjoyed Hooch, Reef and vodka a little too much and it would mean that I'd get literally blind drunk and not be able to even see boys, let alone date them. But it was ok. I was ok. I was having the best fun EVER.

Then in my final year, I realized I actually quite fancied a boy I had lived with in my first year. Lewis.

We'd been best mates for the full three years. He was a proper player. And rugby player. So he was a big hit with the girls. He was from Rochdale. One night – and I still actually have no idea to this day how – I ended up in bed with him. I remember waking up one morning and thinking, oh shit, I'm in Lewis' bed, and I'm naked.

I'd stayed with him often because he loved drinking as much as I did so we often got smashed then crashed. But this time it was different. I could tell by the nakedness. AGH! I got up in a panic and left. When I got home and confessed to my mates, they were all so excited. They had wanted it to happen for ages.

I waited all day to hear from him… nothing.

So I decided to text him… asking if he was ok with what had happened, if he thought it could be something we could do again and if we could actually be together. I pressed send and turned up my Stereophonics album *Just Enough Education to Perform*. I then began to clean my room – something I did not do often but which was a good distraction while I waited for the reply.

I distinctly remember his reply.

Lewis: Shel, I love you like I love a sister, you know this. I think the world of you, however I can't manage to look after myself and you deserve someone better than me. Sorry xxx

I was so gutted. I was angry. I'd become just another girl he'd slept with.

I can't really remember what happened the next time I saw him as I obviously turned back to my old mate, vodka. But nothing ever happened between us again. However, to this day, he remains one of my good mates. In fact, I'm sure he'll feature again later...

So I finished uni as a single girl. But most of my friends were in relationships by then. As were all of my sisters.

How hard could it be?

Chapter Two

I had been working at a local radio station in Manchester from the age of 15 and I managed to get more work back there after uni.

I used to think: maybe I'll meet a famous pop star, we'll fall in love and I'll live happily ever after as a teeny bopper.

But the reality was that aside from working every hour under the sun, the main thing I did was go out, have fun and get blind drunk. I figured that I might as well focus on having fun, rather than pulling boys. So I did.

They were the best years of my life.

I met my best mate Lucy at the radio station. We became inseparable. She loved vodka as much as me and, together, we learnt to love sambuca! We'd go on crazy holidays to Ibiza every year and go away for weekends. There wasn't a weekend that we didn't do something crazy. (By the way, this is not where I confess my undying love for her and reveal that we're now living happily ever after together!)

When we were out, I'd manage to have the odd cheeky snog with a rugby player, or guys we had got to know on the clubbing scene in Manchester. But it never amounted to anything more and I never managed to get a boyfriend. Though to be honest, I don't think I really wanted one. I definitely didn't need one.

When I turned 24, Lucy announced she was going to go travelling for six months and asked if I wanted to join her. But I had worked so hard to get my job in radio that I was scared to leave it. So she went on her own. What was I going to do for six months without her?

We spoke every day. I was working an overnight shift so the time difference meant we were both awake at the same time. She was having the greatest time ever, and I was spending every day sitting in a studio, working. I was bored and becoming boring.

Lucy set me a challenge: 'By the time I get back from Australia, you will not still be sitting in that studio.'

So I started applying for jobs all over the country. They were still in radio because it was all I knew how to do having drunk my way through university and missed out on learning anything useful.

I sent letters to every radio station in the UK using different coloured paper so that I stood out (original, I know.) I had a few interviews but they didn't go anywhere. As time went by, it got closer to when Lucy was due to return and I started to worry less about completing her challenge because I knew my pal would be back and the fun could restart.

Not long after she returned, we went to Ibiza on our annual trip and one afternoon, my phone rang. I was a bit tipsy so answered without looking who it was.

'Hello, can I speak to Shelly please?'

'Shelly speaking,' I slurred out.

'It's David here. I'd like to offer you the job.'

SHIT SHIT SHIT.

I had applied for a job in Cardiff. A job I really didn't know how to do. Or really what it was. But somehow, I'd got it. AGHHH.

I was so shocked. I told him I was in Ibiza but I would be home in three days and would call him back. I went out to Lucy – who I'd locked out on the balcony so that I could concentrate on the call – and told her the news. We were both so excited but OMG what was I going to do? Cardiff? I'd never even been to Cardiff!

Lucy convinced me it was such a good opportunity that I had to take it. So we went out to buy some cheap fizz and started celebrating. But later that night, when I was really drunk, the reality hit me and I cried, and cried and cried. Did I really want to do this? Move to a city I didn't know, in another country (ok, it's only Wales but they do have their own language!) and without Lucy?

Anyway, it turned out that accepting the job in Cardiff was the best decision of my life so far.

Within a few weeks, Lucy found out she'd also got a new job in Sheffield so we would both be moving away. It would mean I wasn't going to be jealous of any new friends that Lucy might find in Manchester, having fun without me.

So off I went to Cardiff. In my little silver Saxo with my life packed in the back. I listened to Jack Johnson all the way there and cried with fear and panic.

*****

I fell in love immediately with Cardiff, with Wales, with the people. It was amazing.

I quickly realized I could actually do the job – and pretty well as it turned out – and I loved everything about it. I soon became great friends with people from work and started to enjoy my new life. Obviously, I continued my love of vodka and sambuca. And I often made journeys to Sheffield to see Lucy or she'd come to see me and we'd still talk every day on the phone – we often called just to watch *Corrie* together.

Life was great.

One day at work, I noticed a new girl sitting at her desk reading some kind of book that she was trying to hide under the table. How odd, I thought. What could it be?

I had liked this new girl from the day she started. Very pretty, big eyes, very silly personality – my kind of silly. The kind of girl who has no idea how beautiful she is and how the room lights up the moment she enters. She's one of THEM. The kind of girl I'd love to be. I decided that I may not be able to be her, but I could try and befriend her.

The next time I came out of my studio, I saw her again, book on lap but under the table. I went to ask. She awkwardly looked up at me, checked me out for a moment as if she was working out if she could trust me, if I was the kind of girl who would understand. Then, she simply smiled, closed the book and showed me the front cover.

The Complete Book of Rules: Time-tested secrets for capturing the heart of Mr Right by Ellen Fein and Sherrie Schneider.

I did a little squeal with excitement. Amazing. I KNEW we should be friends.

Simone was dating a man called Will. Will was perfect but she was terrified that she may lose him so she was using every possible (working) hour reading this book in the hope that she'd capture his heart.

In my head all I could think was if Simone needed to read a book to keep a man – and she is BEAUTIFUL – then maybe I'd be ok? Maybe I just needed to read the book? Maybe this was going to save my love life! According to the front cover, it's 'the notorious dating handbook which has changed the life of millions'. I wanted to become a 'Rules Girl'.

We continued our conversation in my soundproof studio so she could tell me the basic rules:

1. Don't call him – it will make him desire you more.
2. Always end the date first – it will leave them desperate for more.
3. Don't call back immediately if he does call you. You are a VERY busy girl.
4. End the first call after 15 minutes.
5. Don't reveal too much information in date one.
6. Refrain from seeing him 2–3 times a week to begin with.
7. Be busy until the date. Busy people are important. You want to be important.
8. Even if you're not busy, pretend you are.
9. DO NOT SLEEP WITH THEM ON DATE ONE.
10. Be aloof.

From this point onwards, I decided I would apply The Rules to everyone. Ha! This was going to change everything.

*****

Simone and I became very good friends. We often went to Nando's to discuss The Rules. But we would end up drinking way too much wine and then spend the rest of the evening trying not to break any of the rules, which is pretty tricky after one too many.

The other problem was that I continued to have appalling skills when it came to pulling boys. On nights out, I'd manage to have the odd snog with a handsome Welshman but it never seemed to lead to anything more.

Rhodri was a close call.

I'd seen him out a few times but the final time, I'd had one too many Jägerbombs – although in those days I don't even think they were called that. They were just an horrific drink that used to make me sick. Very sick. And I was NEVER EVER EVER sick. I could drink and drink and somehow never be sick. Until now.

I'd gone back to Rhodri's flat at the end of the night and I must have passed out. When I woke up, I was naked. All I could think was:

Uh oh, I feel very sick.

No it's ok, I'm never sick.

No I definitely feel sick.

Oh god yes.

I'm 100 per cent going to be sick.

So I jumped up and ran out of his room. But then I suddenly realised I had no idea where his bathroom was. I opened every door until I found it, literally just in time. Boy, was I sick.

After about ten minutes I heard a voice ask if I was ok. I turned around and to my horror… IT WASN'T RHODRI. It was his flat mate. I didn't even know he had a flat mate. So not only was this stranger seeing me naked, he was also seeing me vom. Nice.

Once I'd managed to pull myself together and leave, I never heard from Rhodri again. To my friends, he has the name Naked Sick Boy.

Chapter Three

On a work night out when I was 26, I somehow ended up snogging a guy from the office. Ed.

Ed who worked in the studio in front of mine. I used to see the back of his head every day. The snogging became a bit of a regular thing. Very regular in fact.

So, one night I decided to ask him if perhaps there could be more to it than just snogging.

He said no.

WHAT?

He said he was sorry to have led me on but he just wanted a bit of fun and didn't want anything serious. I was so shocked because he was such a nice guy.

Not one to give up easily, I told him to have a think about it. I said I would go for a wee, and when I came back, I would ask him again. Which I did. In fact, I did this five times over the course of the night. This night became infamous as 'the night of the five last chances'. I knew this was pretty much breaking every rule in the goddamn book. This was the least aloof I'd ever been. I HATE THE RULES.

Sadly though, every time, his answer was the same.

So I had to get a grip and pretend it never happened, which by then, I was becoming pretty good at.

Anyway, despite the awkwardness, we stayed friends and all was ok.

Until one night, when another one of my new friends, Sally, had a word with him. Sally did not like The Rules at all. She asked Ed why he wasn't interested in me because apparently I'm a 'good catch'. It was like we were 15.

He confessed to her that he'd made a massive mistake and he had wanted to tell me that, in fact, he did like me and did want to give it a go but he was scared.

Sally, in no uncertain terms, told him to man up. So he did… by downing about eight pints before coming to talk to me.

I was so angry that I stormed out without saying anything. How dare he think he can just tell me he does like me and expect me to say, 'Ok, that's brilliant'. Obviously, that's exactly what I wanted to say but this was playing the rules! I WIN! So now he'll fall in love with me, right?

I ignored him and the whole issue for a week. Rules Girls don't call the guys, so I waited out.

However, by the following weekend on (yet) another night out, we had words and I told him I guess I could allow him just one, final, last chance. We had a cheeky snog in the back of a taxi – again like we were 15.

*****

Ed and I ended up dating for years. Over five years in fact.

I finally had an actual long-term boyfriend! My family and work colleagues were overjoyed because it meant I wasn't a lesbian, which they were all convinced I was.

But, sadly, it didn't work out. Relationships are all about quality not quantity and if I'm honest, it wasn't working for a large part of those five years.

Ed was – and is – a very lovely guy. We remain good friends, and I believe we always will be, but he was basically a bit emotionally retarded. In all the time we were together, he was unable to tell me he loved me, that I looked nice, and was reluctant to tell people he had a girlfriend. Ed hid anything on Facebook that suggested he had a girlfriend and DEFINITELY didn't want to add 'in a relationship' to his profile.

Once, at a party, he actually got my name wrong and introduced me to his friends as Sally. I mean, yes, it's close to Shelly but it's not right and names are pretty fundamental!

He was also a massive commitmentphobe.

After two years of being together, I needed somewhere new to live. So, I suggested that maybe we should consider moving in together. He FREAKED out and told me he'd 'get back to me'.

He never did.

A few years later I asked again.

Still the same response.

Obviously, we saw each other every day at work but outside the office, I only used to see him on a Wednesday evening and on some weekends. He couldn't handle the thought of being with me for any longer because that was way too serious.

On the rare occasions that I would stay over, he would freak out if I left shower gel or my toothbrush at his house. I would get into work to discover he'd brought them in and put them on my desk.

We never went on holiday together. In five years! Why? Because he didn't 'like' holidays. WHO DOESN'T LIKE HOLIDAYS?

I realised that his work was more of a priority in his life than me. One New Year's Eve, I even said to him, 'I wish you loved me and gave me the attention that you give to that light projector'.

True story. I realised the relationship – if you can call it that – was making me massively unhappy.

*****

I'd started running to keep myself occupied in all the time I wasn't spending with Ed. It gave me something to do apart from sitting at home hoping he'd call and suggest we go out. (We also never went on a date either.)

Like a lot of people do, I got a little obsessed with running because it was making me feel great. I was losing weight like you wouldn't believe. I signed up to do 5k races, then 10k races but every single one I went to on my own. I ran on my own, picked my medal up on my own and walked home on my own because Ed would always have been out drinking the night before and couldn't get out of bed to support me.

I bravely decided to sign up to do a half marathon. I trained and trained. Three weeks before, Ed had been out drinking (again) and had come to stay at mine because it was close to the bar he'd been in. He was snoring so loudly and stank of booze. Just as I finally managed to get to sleep as the sun was coming up, a group of seagulls started making one hell of a noise right outside my window. In a sleep-deprived rage, I got out of bed to shout at the seagulls and bashed my knee so hard on the corner of my wooden bed frame. It properly hurt. I was gutted. I didn't want to pull out of the half marathon and I couldn't – I had raised over £800 for charity – I had to do it. So, I continued to run through the pain but that just caused more injury.

All this just added to my unhappiness.

One day in the gym, Christina Aguilera's *The Voice Within* came on my iPod Shuffle and I realised my voice within was saying I had to get out.

But that was easier said than done.

For weeks, I would drive to his house and call Lucy on the way telling her I was definitely going to do it. She'd tell me it was for the best and wish me good luck. We must have had this conversation SO many times. But every time, I would text her the next day to say I hadn't done it. Truth was, I didn't want to face it. I didn't want that awful sad conversation.

Anyway, one day (and I don't really know what clicked in my head to make it any different to the other times), I just did. I guess I just knew I HAD to do it as I was desperately unhappy.

It still turns my stomach now to think about it. He cried. He actually cried. It was the most emotion he had shown in five years. But it was awful. He said how sorry he was and how he knew I deserved better than him and he hated himself for not being able to give me more and show me more love. But he said that was just how he was and who he is. Awful, awful, awful.

I cried for weeks trying to work out why someone couldn't show me their love. Was it me? Was there something wrong with me? It was a truly horrible time.

The Rules had failed me. I quit The Rules. They suck.

Chapter Four

18 months after Ed and I split up, I was still single.

Despite trying, I had failed to find anyone else. I never was good at going out and flirting – I'm not sure if I mentioned this?

Ed and I were still close though and so we decided to give it another go.

It was great to begin with but soon the reality hit home that he was just the same: in his own little world and nothing had changed. Over the course of a year (yes, it took a whole year!), we discovered that we really wanted different things. I wanted a husband, kids, and a family. He did not.

During this time, I started working with a guy called Mark. He was in a relationship very similar to mine and Ed's, but it was the opposite way round. His girlfriend never paid him compliments, clearly had commitment issues and didn't want to go on holiday with him. We had a lot in common.

We got to a point where we'd chat a couple of times a week about our crap relationships. Mark would tell me that I was worth more and would try to make me see that Ed was wrong for me. I of course was giving him the same advice back – did he really think she was his only chance of happiness?

We were going round and round in circles moaning about our less than perfect significant others. But hearing him constantly moan made me realise that I also needed to stop moaning. It was obvious to me that Mark wasn't with the right person and he kept saying that he could see Ed wasn't right for me.

As we spoke more, I started to question... was Mark the right person?! Talking to him helped build my confidence. Was it slapping me in the face this whole time? (What I should perhaps tell you is that Mark was ever so handsome.)

No. Looks aside, he wasn't right. I told myself I couldn't think like that because I was still with Ed and committed to Ed. Even though he didn't want to commit to me.

But the more Mark and I spoke, the closer we got. Not physically obviously but just emotionally, in a way I'd never felt close to Ed and in a strange way, I started to feel like I was almost cheating on Ed. Probably sounds stupid since all Mark and I had done was talk – and mostly on the phone.

Mark lived in London so I only ever saw him if I was working there which wasn't very often. But when I did go, Mark would always take me out for lunch. I'd feel like a giggly schoolgirl. He knew how to say things to make me feel better. He would tell me that my boyfriend had no idea how lucky he was and that I really could do better.

If we ever accidentally touched feet under a table or brushed past each other, I got a sense of excitement, of butterflies. It was a feeling I had not had for years.

But one day, it became clear that Mark was having similar thoughts.

'I think I fancy you' he said.

I didn't know what to say. A part of me wanted to say it

back. But I couldn't. It felt wrong. I loved Ed. Despite all his flaws, I was in love with him... or so I thought.

I told Mark to shut up and joked that he was only allowed to say that when we were living together and engaged to be married. But we then continued to joke about this ridiculous scenario for weeks, maybe months.

When Mark would tell me that I should break up with Ed, leave Cardiff and move to London to be with him, I'd laugh and point out that despite the huge logistical effort required for that to happen, there was of course the small matter of Mark's girlfriend.

I did start looking at jobs in London though. In a strange way, I hoped that if I told Ed I was thinking of moving away, he would step up and tell me not to go because of how much he loved me.

It was though, as ever with Ed, a false hope.

Not only did he not declare his undying love and beg me to stay. He encouraged me to go for the jobs. And all that did was make me think more that perhaps Mark's crazy idea wasn't so crazy after all...

Even though nothing ever happened between us, I felt that it was all starting to get a bit messy. The whole situation was starting to give me panic attacks. I used to call Lucy telling her I had pains in my chest and couldn't breathe. She'd have to guide me through breathing into a paper bag to try and calm me down.

However I had got into this, what was clear was that I needed to get out. Staying with Ed was wrong. I was being unfair. I needed to be honest with myself because as much as we got on really well, 'getting on really well' wasn't what I was looking for in a relationship.

By then, I was 32 years old, and didn't have time to be just getting on well with someone. The clock was ticking. It wasn't what I wanted for my life so I had to give up fighting to change Ed and walk away.

So I went through that heartbreak all over again. Awful. You would think that after everything, it would be easier to do it a second time. But if anything it was harder. It properly broke my heart. He didn't fight for me, at all. He literally let me break up with him and walk away.

Seeing him every day in work didn't help. I spent a lot of time sitting in my car in the car park crying. Pathetic, I know.

Luckily, I had amazing friends around who helped to pull me through it. (And my mum on the phone constantly, without whom god knows what mess I'd be in.) My poor Welsh bestie, Sally, dealt with me in some bad states. Once, I cried in New Look on Barry Island because some socks reminded me of Ed. How she didn't say 'get a grip', I have no idea. But she just laughed at me, which made me laugh too. After that, whenever I was with Sally, we would throw shiny five pence pieces into the water in Cardiff Bay, putting wishes on them. I always wished to find someone who loved me, didn't take me for granted, who made me happy and wanted to be with me forever.

There's a saying: 'Never go back to your ex. It's like reading the same book over and over again when you know how the story ends.' It's so true. Although, I have to say that I don't regret it because I would have always wondered 'what if?' – especially knowing know what was to come next.

*****

Not long after Ed and I called it a day, work offered me the chance to do my job back in Manchester. In my heart,

I really didn't want to leave what had become my new home. I'd grown to LOVE Wales, the life I'd created for myself, the friends I'd made.

But it soon became apparent that if I didn't move back to Manchester, I'd lose my job and radio was still all I knew. So I guess I was forced into the decision. I was properly gutted. Nine years of my life I'd spent in Cardiff and I felt I had to give it all up.

The worst thing was that I only had two weeks to do it. I found out it was 'now or never' and then had to pack up my life, hire a van and leave Cardiff. God, that was tough.

But looking back, it was the best thing for my heart. Being away from that life with Ed in it, starting a completely new life back in Manchester helped me mend myself. One of my favourite quotes really helped get me through that time: 'If you spend too long holding onto the one who treats you like an option, you will miss finding someone who treats you as a priority.'

I was going back to my family, to Lucy (who had also moved back home), and all my other friends.

It was all going to be ok.

Chapter Five

Six months after I'd moved back to Manchester, having settled into my new flat, and got to grips with my new job, I decided it was time to get back out there and discover what Manchester had to offer in the way of potential boyfriends.

I have three sisters, two of whom are married and the other is in a long-term relationship. So all eyes were on me to meet someone.

'If Rachel can find someone online, surely you can too,' they said.

Rachel had recently got married, having met her lovely, normal husband on eHarmony three years before.

I had always said I would never do online dating. I had always felt that I didn't need to go online to meet someone. It just wasn't for me. I would simply go out and meet someone in a traditional way.

Nope, online dating was 100 per cent not for me.

Noooo wayyyyy.

Never.

Well, obviously, I gave in.

It didn't take me long. I opened the app store on my phone

and terrifyingly typed in the word 'Tinder'. Here goes nothing, I thought.

It blew my mind.

It's like snap.

But the worst game of snap you've ever played.

There are men. Many men. Some with photos of them with tigers, some with elephants. Some at festivals, some climbing mountains, most of them snowboarding. Then there are some with group photos so you have no idea which one you're playing snap with.

I decided it was kind of like being in a pub. You scan the room and choose who you fancy. The bonus with this though is that you already know they're all single (well, you kind of hope they are).

Each profile that comes up, you either swipe left if you're not interested or right if you are. Then, when you do swipe right, there's the agony of waiting a few seconds to see if we have matched? Did he swipe right too?

'Don't judge a book by its cover,' is what is drummed into us from a young age but this is 100 per cent judging men from just five photos. I would judge them on their friends in the photo or what they were wearing. I decided that if there were too many photos of them wearing sunglasses, they must be hiding wonky eyes or if they were smiling with their mouth closed, they must have horrific teeth or none at all. The men whose pictures were purely selfie photos must have no friends to take photos for them and therefore they must be weird.

But off I went, swiping left and right. If I'm honest, I rarely swiped right due to my massively judgemental ways.

When you do get a match though, it's exciting! If your phone isn't on silent, you get a lovely little sound and a lovely notification to say, 'It's a Match!' You then have the option to either send them a message or 'Keep Playing'. Playing? This is not a game! This is my life! I decided I should send messages. Why wouldn't I?

Problem is, no one responds to messages. So you go from an instant 'Ooooooh exciting, he likes me!' to 'Oh, he's a non-replier'. It's an emotional rollercoaster, I tell you.

Next time I had a match, I didn't send a message. I decided maybe men didn't like that, so I waited... AND HE MESSAGED ME!

Matt. Firefighter. Lives around the corner. Also 32 years old.

OMG. What do I do now? I'm talking to a random man off the internet. EEK!

Chapter Six

We chatted for a few days. He seemed normal and funny. I asked if he'd braved any Tinder dates?

'No,' he said. 'I'm trying to ask one girl out but she's not taking the hints.'

'Just ask her,' I replied. 'Maybe she's a bit stupid?'

'OK, will you come on a date with me?'

OMG he was talking about me? My mind went into overdrive.

I can't possibly meet a random man off the internet. From an app? Off Tinder? Everyone says the men are just after one thing! Why did I even sign up to this? Oh lord. What now? Do I go?

I panicked. A lot. I screenshot his photo and sent it to ALL my friends asking if he looked like a murderer. They all told me to just do it. Why not?

We added each other on Facebook, which made me feel better about him. It meant I could see more photos of him, posts he'd been tagged in when out with his mates, etc. It was going to be ok. So I said yes.

He asked if I was free the following night. I said no.

Obviously, I was free but I was not ready for this. I needed to sit and worry about it for days first. (And, of course, I like to think I still play by The Rules and this is exactly what a Rules Girl would do.)

Four days later, on a Sunday night, my sister dropped me at the train station where I was meeting him outside. She was going to check him out before I got out of the car. She did enough internet dating herself to be able to spot a weirdo. I felt sick. What was I doing? I didn't need the internet to find a man. Surely I could just go to a bar and talk to men? Surely?

I got out of the car. Shaking. I had not been on a date in what felt like FOREVER. I panicked. What happens? It's 2014, do men still pay? Do we eat? Do I drink alcohol? How much alcohol do I drink? What do we talk about? Do I need prepared questions?

Anyway, I needn't have worried. The date was bloody brilliant.

We went to a restaurant, sat across a table from each other, chatted, had a laugh. Because Ed and I had never really been on dates, it was nice to sit with a man for so long and just talk. We discussed what we fancied off the menu, which wine we fancied to SHARE. Even that got me excited! We had banter with the waiters and other couples in the restaurant. THIS was what I wanted in life: a man who clearly enjoyed my company and could hold himself well on a date.

Matt was so handsome. He was very tall (again, the complete opposite to Ed) and his lovely toned arms were on show under a tight short-sleeved polo neck. I could smell his amazing aftershave every time he used his hands whilst talking. He had something about him. He was ever so confident with a cheeky personality. I liked it. It was a nice change. He was interested in me, in my job, my family, my life in Cardiff.

THIS WAS FUN! Who knew?! Why had I waited so long to go online?

After we had eaten, he suggested we went to another pub for one more drink. However, that one more drink turned into a pub crawl. Turned out dates weren't so scary at all. I could do this! Admittedly, I don't really remember the last bar but I just remember laughing a lot and almost falling off a chair (before realising it was Sunday and I had to go to work in the morning).

When the end of the night came (purely because every bar and pub was closing), we walked to the taxi queue. It was a bit awkward because we lived quite close to each other. He would have to drive down my road, past my flat, to get to his place, so it made sense that we shared a taxi. But this concerned me.

Although I was not used to dates – especially dates with strangers – what I did know was that it's not cool to sleep with someone on a first date. So I had to make it 100 per cent clear that I was getting out at mine and he was going to carry on in the taxi. He agreed to this so I needn't have panicked. But once we were in the taxi and almost at my place, Matt realised he'd lost his wallet. I only had enough money to get to mine so couldn't help him out. He told me it was ok because he was a big lad and he'd walk the rest of the way home as it wasn't that far (I'm sure it's about another two miles but I wasn't going to argue). He made it out it was something he does often so we got out of the taxi outside my flat. But then, he asked if he could use my toilet before he set off.

'Oh,' I said. 'Like that is it? That's how you think you're going to get into my flat? No way, you can pee in a bush on the road!'

'I can't do that!!' he said. 'I'm a big guy, I'll be seen and you don't want a neighbour seeing someone you know taking

29

a wee against their trees. I'll literally nip in and then leave. I promise.'

What could I say? 'Ok then, but you're leaving straight after you've used the bathroom.'

Luckily I had cleaned and tidied my flat otherwise there really was no way I'd have let him in at all. I decided to stand in my lounge with my coat on and be as uninviting as possible until he left. I heard the toilet flush and the taps go and I suddenly started to get nervous.

At first I didn't know why – I'd just had a lovely evening with a lovely man. But then it dawned. He was a total stranger. As if I'd let a total stranger into my house. WHAT WAS I THINKING? The bathroom door opened and he came into the lounge where we stood, awkwardly making conversation about the photographs on my wall. He then finally said, 'Right then, I best be off. Leave you to your beauty sleep.'

And then he leant down to kiss me. It was so lovely. So so lovely. To be kissed by a) an amazing kisser and b) someone who really wants to kiss me after such a long time was so good. We kissed for a while until I managed to say, 'You really should leave'.

'I know' he said and then he kissed me some more.

*****

I woke up the following morning to discover I was still drunk in bed. And there was a man next to me. Oh bugger. This was NOT meant to happen. I don't do this! HE IS A STRANGER! HE COULD HAVE MURDERED ME! I then had a word with myself because I was pretty sure that although I was still drunk, I was alive. He did not murder me. PHEW.

I didn't know what to do. He was properly asleep. All

handsome and asleep. IN MY BED. No one had been in my bed other than me. I lay very still for a while. Then it hit me.

SHIT!

IT'S MONDAY!

I have to go to work!

I jumped up and got in the shower. The whole time I was in the shower, I was wondering if he'd still be in my flat when I got out. I delicately walked back into my bedroom to discover him awake, dressed and lying on top of my bed (which he'd made) looking at his phone.

'Morning.'

'Morning,' he replied. 'I promise that I did mean to leave after I used the bathroom.'

I just laughed and told him to shut up, then tried to get ready for work… with a handsome man watching me. Weird.

I offered him breakfast but he said he'd get something on his walk home, because he genuinely did mean it when he said he was going to walk. So, as I went down to my car, he walked with me, gave me a kiss and told me to text him and to have a nice day. Weird. Again.

I then watched him walk off. All tall and handsome and confident. That man had spent the night with me. This was madness.

*****

Matt wanted to see me again that night but I had plans. They were with Lucy and our friend Jude to have a 'debrief' on the date. So I saw him on the Tuesday.

I told him I was training for a 10k and would need to go for a run before I met him so asked if we could meet about 8pm. I needed to give myself enough time to stop sweating and for my red face to calm down.

Instead, he suggested we run together because he was a runner too. WIN! Well, it was a win that he was a runner but I wasn't sure yet if it was a win that we were going to run together on our second date. I'm really not very good. And I'm really not very fast, at all. But I decided that maybe it was the perfect second date. At least he'd see me at my very worst and if he still liked me after that then it'd be a bonus. He had also suggested that he'd cook for me afterwards and his suggestion was sausage and mash – one of my all time favourites! Could this guy be any more perfect?

I then had the sudden panic of WHAT ON EARTH WILL I WEAR? Ok, it would have to be my running gear, but I was not sure I was ready for him to see me in Lycra. (Yes, I know he probably saw me in nothing two nights before but I chose to ignore that fact.)

What if he runs behind me watching my bum wobble, I thought. That is NOT attractive. AGH! Maybe I should cancel?

I saw him arrive at my flat and get out of his car wearing red shorts and a black t-shirt. The butterflies in my stomach went crazy.

'Ok,' I told myself. 'Must stay cool and calm.'

I opened the door to him, he gave me a kiss on the cheek and said, 'Ready to rock and roll? I've looked at a map and found a nice four-mile loop round here. Let's do this!'

FOUR miles?

I had a minor panic but decided it would be good. He would be pushing me past my three-mile comfort zone and I did need to crank it up. He offered to carry my keys, which was ever so gentlemanly of him, and off we went.

He was ahead of me the entire time (no surprise there) but it actually kept me running. I always have a constant battle in my head when running – I call it my running chimp. It's like there's a naughty chimp sat on my shoulder telling me to stop. But that chimp was not there. It was a giggly chimp instead.

Ha, I thought to myself, I'm literally chasing after a hot man!

Look at me, running with a guy, I smiled. We look like a couple! I'd be jealous of us if I past us in a car.

The even greater thing was he really had looked at a map and took me down lovely leafy roads and paths that I didn't know existed so close to my home. It was so thoughtful. It really was all I'd ever dreamt of.

He told me over dinner that he was so confident in him and I that he had deleted Tinder off his phone. He didn't want to meet anyone else now he'd found me.

I had to keep checking there was nothing nearby that he could use to whack me over the head and kill me with.

'Are you really not a murderer?' I asked him over and over. He would just laugh and say, 'Not yet'.

I decided there MUST be something wrong with him. Surely internet dating wasn't as easy as: chat to one man, go on a date with one man, marry that one man?

Chapter Seven

Date three was planned for the Friday of the same week, three days later. The plan was to go for some food, then go and play crazy golf in the Trafford Centre. I was excited.

It had started to feel like I had a boyfriend, even though it had been less than a week since I had met him. That night, I rushed home from work, decided what to wear and put on a bit of eyeliner. (I'm not much of a makeup wearer so eyeliner was me making a lot of effort.) Matt was coming to pick me up at 7pm.

I got a text from him at 6.40pm:

Matt: Been called out on a job, will be running a bit late, I'll keep you updated.

As he was a firefighter, I was aware that from time to time, his job might mean that he couldn't be as flexible as he wanted. It's not like if there's a huge fire, he can just say, 'Sorry guys, I'm gonna have to leave you to this, I've got a date'. So it was fine.

He then called me at 7pm to tell me that he was really sorry but he wouldn't be able to come. They had got to the call-out and there was no fire but a dead body and so he had to stay with the body until the police and ambulance arrived.

Wow. Drama. It certainly put my life and my job into perspective. I told him it was ok and not to worry, that obviously I was gutted but I understood and we could just rearrange.

The following day, I was off to London because Lucy was running the London Marathon. It's something I plan to do one day, but this year I was going to watch her do it. So Matt and I decided we'd see each other on the Sunday when I was back.

I woke up to a text from him on Saturday morning. He had sent it late at night when he had got in from work, apologizing for cancelling on me. I replied telling him not to worry at all and asked what his plans for the day were. He didn't reply. That was ok though, he didn't have to reply immediately.

I got on a train with Lucy and all her family and off we went to London. Lucy's sister was asking me all about Matt – they were all as excited as my family that maybe I'd finally met someone who was right for me. I tried to play it down but I think my inner giddiness gave it away so I decided to show her some photos of him on Facebook.

The problem was that I could no longer see his Facebook page. I couldn't even find him on there. Bit weird but I decided it was probably a bad network on the train and I'd show her later.

After watching Lucy WIN the London Marathon on Sunday (ok, that's a slight exaggeration but she did amazingly better than I ever could), we all piled back on the train home. I still couldn't see Matt's Facebook profile so I decided to text him. It wouldn't deliver. So I called him and it went straight to his answer phone. I left a message:

'Hi Matt, it's me, just checking you're ok as I can't seem

to get through to you? Hope you're ok and have had a nice weekend.'

Nothing. I got nothing. I couldn't understand? Maybe he'd lost his phone? Yes! It must be that...

It got to Monday night and I decided to send him a message because it finally dawned on me that he'd blocked me on Facebook, and on his phone. It was the only thing that made sense. Well, it didn't make any sense at all. Why would he do that?

Me: Hey. I'm not really sure what has happened. It seems you have blocked me from your phone and on all forms of social media. I don't understand as everything seemed to be going really well even though it's only been a week. I feel like we've got a true connection and that this could be something, but you've disappeared. I hope you receive this text as I'd really like to talk to you. Hope you're ok. Shel xxxx

About three days later I got a message on Facebook from him:

Matt: Hiya. I don't understand what has happened? We seemed to be getting on really well. I thought we were going to go on another date. I really like you Shelly but it looks like you've blocked me? Please can you let me know what's going on? Hope you're ok x

WHAT?!

That was pretty much the same message I had sent to him! I replied instantly telling him that but he didn't get my message. How ODD. Really, really ODD!

He then asked if I was free that night so we went for a drink. Apart from trying to work out what on earth happened with Facebook, we seemed to just pick up where we had left off on our last date. So we continued to see each other, going for roast dinners on Sundays and running together (he got me up to 10k! Amazing!). Everything was brilliant.

*****

After just three weeks, I decided to introduce Matt to my mates. The night he was due to meet them, he had football training so I left him in my flat and he planned to meet us about 8pm. When I got to the pub, EVERYONE was asking about him. They wanted to know EVERYTHING and were excited to meet him.

Everyone except one of my cynical friends, Claire. She was concerned. (She's been married for seven years and she and her husband have been together for eleven years in total so she does not understand or trust online daters.) She kept saying that she couldn't believe I'd left a total stranger in my flat with all my belongings including the keys to my car. I told her he was not a stranger, I had known him for three weeks! Ok, I know that's not long at all but I just knew he wasn't dodgy and wasn't going to screw me over.

But then it got to 8.30pm and he still wasn't there. I called him. No answer. It then got to 9pm and I started to feel sick. I had trusted a total stranger with my life.

He's robbing me as I'm sitting in the pub isn't he? I thought. I've fallen for this. He's been building this relationship for three weeks to make me trust him so he can steal my car and all my belongings!

Oh god, oh god, oh god. What on earth had I done? Why

was I so stupid? Who trusts someone after three weeks? Me! I do! What an idiot.

I didn't know what to do. I could call the police but I had willingly left my keys with this man. This was the kind of story you hear on the news: 'Shelly Smith from Manchester fell into the online dating trap of a man and allowed him to rob her.'

All manner of things were going through my head about what was actually in my flat, when suddenly there he was!

At the bar! Ordering ten Jägerbombs as an introduction from him to my mates. PHEW. YESSSS, I knew I could trust him! Claire and everyone else had made me doubt him. The poor man! Thank god for that. Wow. That was an awful 45 minutes.

Everyone instantly loved him (who doesn't love a man with free Jägerbombs?). He was funny, charming, handsome, cheeky. He was a hit. It was so, so perfect and I was so happy. I never thought this was possible. I sat and watched him work the room in disbelief that he was mine. He'd catch my eye from time to time and give me a little wink that gave me butterflies.

The greatest feeling was knowing that for the first time in a long while, when all my mates left the pub to go home to their boyfriends/husbands, I too would be going home to someone. I was going home with Matt, and I'd be waking up with him in the morning. There was no better feeling.

Chapter Eight

Matt started staying over more and more. It was quite tricky to see him otherwise due to his shift work.

He'd started doing lovely little things like if he had left at 5am, when I'd get up, there'd be a bowl and spoon out on the side ready for my cereal and he'd have written a little note and put it in the bowl. Just simple things like, 'Have a nice day' or 'Can't wait to see you later'. I decided that since they made me super happy each morning, I wanted to do it back. So I bought some *Juicy Lucy Little Box of Cheeky Chat Ups* cards that are funny and cute. They are small enough to put in a wallet or pocket, which is generally where I'd hide them.

I cleared out a drawer for him in my bedroom, he came to a friend's Christening with me, we booked a camping weekend away with Lucy and her boyfriend… it was all my dreams come true. All these things I'd wanted to do for years but had had to do them alone, I now had someone to do them with. We planned a holiday to Croatia, he took me back to his home town up in the Lakes. It couldn't be more perfect.

Until stuff started getting weird.

There were periods when I'd not be able to get hold of

him for a day or so. And he'd keep disappearing off social media. I also realised he never told me when he had found the little cards I'd been hiding in his clothes. One day, when I was out running, he happened to drive past me even though I hadn't told him I was going for a run and I was down a lane that generally people don't drive down as it doesn't take you anywhere.

Some mornings I'd wake up to find him not in bed and he'd either be sitting in the chair in my bedroom fully clothed just watching me, or he'd be in my lounge sat on the sofa in silence. When I'd ask him if he was ok, he'd tell me he didn't think he could be in this relationship. I constantly asked him why and he told me it was complicated, that he had issues with trust and he was scared because he and I were turning into something and he was scared of getting hurt. I had to reassure him that I was scared too and that I knew how important trust was and that I'd never lie to him.

One morning, I woke up to him leaving my flat. I asked him where he was going. It was 3am.

'I can't do this Shelly,' he said. 'I can't. I'm sorry.' And he left.

I was not letting this happen. No way. Not without an explanation. So I got in my car in my pyjamas and drove to his flat as fast as I could. I called him over and over. He obviously didn't answer. I rang and rang and rang. I left voicemails.

Finally, he came down and got in my car.

'I know about the other men, Shelly.'

He went on, 'I knew I couldn't trust you, I knew it. Why would you do this to me?'

I was gobsmacked. What on earth was he talking about? I asked what men he was talking about; there were no other men. He said he'd had a message on Facebook warning him about me. I told him whoever had sent it was clearly mental as there were no other men. I got my phone out and told him to look through it. No messages, nothing. Not even any dating apps.

Who would message him such a thing, I thought? And why? I didn't know anyone crazy enough to do that. He said he had promised the guy that contacted him that he'd never tell me he'd been in touch so refused to tell me where this ridiculous information had come from.

It took a week or so of me convincing him it was nonsense before he'd see me again. But as soon as I did anything nice for him, he'd think it was because I'd cheated. This wasn't a life I could live, being constantly accused of something just because I'm nice.

One evening, I got stuck in traffic coming home from work so I was 15 minutes later than normal. When I pulled into my car park, Matt was sitting in his car waiting for me. He got out and slammed the door shut asking where I'd been.

'Erm, work,' I replied. He asked why I was so late. I told him there had been traffic. He told me it was bullshit and that I'd clearly been to see 'one of my men' on my way home. Again, I had to calm him down and tell him that although he had trust issues, he had to understand that I'd never cheat on him and that he HAD to trust me, otherwise we were not going to work. We decided to go and get a Chinese takeaway and for once take it to his flat in the hope that a change of scenery may help. It didn't help at all. It ended up with me in tears, unable to eat my Chinese because he was repeatedly telling me I was a slag and a slut and that he felt sick just looking at me.

I had done nothing wrong. He told me again that he'd received more messages about me. That he'd been sent screen shots of conversations I'd had with guys. Was I going mad?

Was I having conversations that I'd forgotten about? It got to a point where he was so convincing that I almost started to believe it. He manipulated me so well, made me believe everything he said.

But it got to a point where I could no longer handle it. I told him it had to stop. That we had to stop. We obviously weren't good for each other. He managed to turn it around and be the one who was breaking it off because of my lies.

Even after we'd finished, he would continue to text and email me things, like, 'I hope you had a nice night with Mike, you slag' which I worked out was related to a friend of mine liking my posts on Instagram. Matt had convinced himself that Mike was one of the many men I was seeing behind his back. He would turn up at my flat at 5am before he was going on shift and shout 'coward' up at my window.

A month or so after all of this ended, my sister was getting married to her lovely fiancé who she met on eHarmony. The morning of the wedding, Matt started again with his horrible text messages and they continued throughout the day. I had to give my bag to my dad to look after because I didn't want to see the messages and didn't want him to ruin anything else in my life, especially not my sister's wedding. The next morning he called me to say he knew that I was lying in bed with the best man because I was a slag and that's what slags do.

He turned up at my flat on my 33rd birthday and ruined that as well. He told me he didn't understand why I had so many cards, and why people liked me because all he saw was a horrible person.

He'd go from blocking me on all social media and his phone, to claiming that it was me who had blocked him. Was he dating other women? Was he hiding some kind of secret life? Fact is, I do not know. It really it is still one massive mystery to me.

Unfortunately, I allowed Matt to take over my life for a year. He tormented me for an entire year of my life. My first year back in Manchester. Brilliant start. Luckily, a year on, almost to the day I met him, he moved away to London. It meant I could finally be at peace and try to properly enjoy my Manchester life.

Chapter Nine

Damn.

What now?

Back to Tinder? Or maybe one of the other dating sites? I hadn't got round to any of the others...

My sister met her husband on eHarmony so perhaps that was the place to start.

'People who are willing to pay are serious about wanting to settle down,' everyone in my family kept telling me.

So off I went. I looked at all their offers. I definitely didn't want to sign up for a year! A YEAR? It could take a year? No thanks. So I opted for the lowest price bracket of three months and signed up. £60! But apparently you can't put a price on love...

It was awful. Truly awful. I spent two hours of my life filling in a personality test. But I thought it was worth it, to find my true perfect match.

On eHarmony, you cannot browse the men so I could only see the men that they said were perfect for me.

But if these men were perfect and all that are left, I may as well just sign up to be a spinster on the shelf for life. It was terrible. For two weeks I looked through my matches. How depressing, how totally depressing. I was not attracted to any of my perfect matches, at all. Had I filled something in wrong? Did I give the impression I like large slobs who enjoy spending weekends sitting on the sofa watching American TV boxsets and eating takeaways? I barely even turn my TV on.

So I called eHarmony. And gave them this feedback. I asked for my money back. According to their site, you have a 14-day guarantee. I told them it was a daily disappointment that I could not handle. After being on the phone for twelve minutes and the lady telling me she understands how hard it is to be single and not to give up so quickly, they finally agreed to give me my £60 back. Phew!

Back to Tinder it was then. At least it was a free disappointment.

Within two hours… it popped up: 'It's a Match!' – AND he messaged me.

Here we go again.

*****

Funtime Jim was his name. For two weeks we chatted. We exchanged numbers so we moved off the app onto Whatsapp. How exciting, I thought. He had never met anyone off Tinder before so was as reluctant as I had been. I was at a wedding in Italy – Lake Garda – and it was super romantic. Everyone was in couples and as usual, I was the only single one there. So I decided I needed to up my game with this online dating and actually go on dates again.

Funtime Jim knew I was away and texted me the day I was leaving asking if I'd had a nice time. I told him how it had been the most perfect five days. He then replied with this:

Jim: If you don't want your holiday to end without a holiday romance, when you land, rather than driving home, pop this post code into your satnav and let me take you to dinner WN* *** x

What was I meant I do? Should I meet him? I was driving back from Gatwick so I'd be knackered. And it was really hot back in the UK and I've have been travelling for hours with no air-con in my car. What if I was smelly? I called Lucy. She'd tell me what to do.

Firstly, because she's loads wiser than me, she asked me for the postcode he'd given me as she pointed out that yet again I was being too trusting with a man I'd never met. What if the postcode was his house? And I was going to drive there and get murdered? She confirmed that it was a pub and told me to go for it. Why not? So when I was closer to home, I stopped in a service station to freshen up and to go through my suitcase to decide what I should wear (it was very handy that I had it with me and that I had a fresh tan!).

I had thoroughly stalked him online whilst I was in Italy. I had managed to find him on Facebook even though I only knew his first name (because I've nailed my stalking skills). It seemed typing in his first name, plus the town he's from, plus where he worked was all I needed! Winner! Stalking: complete. And he had an open profile so I could see he was normal, had friends and family. Brilliant!

En route to meet him, my satnav suddenly failed. It told me I had arrived at my destination however I quite clearly hadn't. So I pulled over and text him. He replied saying he lived near the pub so gave me his home postcode and told me to meet him there instead. I instantly called Lucy back. What now? I would really be driving to his house! I gave her the postcode so that at least if he murdered me, she'd be able to tell the police where he lived.

I got the postcode and there he was waiting outside. He said he didn't want me to think it was a ploy to get me inside. So I parked my car and got into his, but as we were going down the road, I noticed some golf clubs in the back.

Uh oh, I thought, he is actually going to murder me, isn't he? He is driving me somewhere to kill me with the golf clubs!

I decided to try and make a joke about it:

'I can't believe I've just got into a stranger's car and I've noticed there are golf clubs in the back. You're going to murder me aren't you?'

He was so sweet.

'Oh god sorry,' he replied. 'I hadn't thought about it, you don't even know my full name. Do you want all my details so you can let someone know? Sorry!'

Little did he know that due to my stalking, I DID know his surname which I'd already given to Lucy and I'd checked him out so I decided I was safe.

Funtime Jim was funny in real life. I was a little concerned from his photos that he may have massive teeth but needn't have worried. They were good, normal, nice teeth. God, he was handsome, he had a great face. We ordered some food and, apart from him accidentally throwing a bowl of peas all over me, it was my first sober date and it was a success.

We decided to meet again but this time he'd come closer to me. We went to my local pub and it was as great as the first date. He made me laugh; he was a true gent. We had things to talk about... another sober success!

But then when it came to date three, he suddenly became much less bothered. His constant excuse was that either the football was on or he was playing football. Or that he was wasted on Jägerbombs. It became obvious to me that he really wasn't interested. So I decided to end that one before it got complicated.

Chapter Ten

SO WHAT NOW?

I decided to brave it and go onto POF (Plenty of Fish).

Now, this dating site is, in fact, a whole other kettle of fish. You can browse and look at any man as many times as you want. There is no swiping. There is just messaging. I hid my profile to begin with, just so I could have a little look – a bit like window-shopping, I guess.

After a few weeks I was feeling brave and clicked 'unhide profile'. BOOM. In came the messages.

But wow – the weirdest men, the weirdest messages. I have decided to share a couple of my favourite messages. Most, I obviously just didn't reply to but some – as you'll see – I thought deserved a simple response. Benji89, I did feel sorry for and Mr RGLM, well, he was ever so attractive…

P5698: Hello how are you. What brings you on here? I'd like to ask you a personal question, please don't be offended... I have just opened a new agency & you would be perfect for it. I could help you earn up to 1500 quid per night if you are interested? xx

KarlyDaddy: Hey beautiful lady. I am at your service. What do you wanna do to me? ;)
Me: Wowzers.

Benji89: Can I tell you a joke & try to make you smile?
Me: Erm... go on then.
Benji89: Well I liked the sound of your profile and look of your photos so thought it would be rude to not try to chat you up? So here goes: what do you call a couple who like to go fishing?
Me: Dunno.
Benji89: You call them Rod and Annette!! Ha!! I know you're laughing deep down! What do you call a seagull on his head?
Me: Don't know...
Benji89: You call him Cliff! Ha! Brilliant again!... a donkey with 3 legs?
Me: Oh god, wow, erm... I don't know.
Benji89: Ha! You can feign grumpy all you want... but you're getting free laughs! Ha!
Me: This is like talking to my Dad...

RGLM: Hey there, you look normal! How are you?
Me: Good thanks, you? Is RGLM your name?
RGLM: Yup! You'll have to guess it...
Me: Roger Lionel Geoffrey MacIntyre?
RGLM: Wow... you're good!
Me: I know!
RGLM: So are you naughty?
Me: Naughty in what way?
RGLM: You tell me...
Me: Oh. You're one of those types aren't you.

Goodniceman: Mmm you look hot! What knickers are you wearing today then sexy? ;)

Jontyjames: What did one ocean say to the other ocean?

RupeRaw: Hi ☺ I was blinded by your beauty so I'm going to require your name and number for insurance purposes haha.

RoysRovers: Your to beautiful for me to know I am just an ordinary guy xxxx Roy xxx

HowieSat: Hi. Do you have any strong opinions on Thai food, rock climbing or camping adventures based around motorbikes? And most importantly... what's your favourite dinosaur...?

James69: Hey, message back if you want to see 9 inches of fun ;)

Richard81: Hi there... how u doing? Wanna meet and spend this weekend together if you like... I live in Manchester and got 2 bedroom apartment.

Hull123: Hello, you ok? What the bloody hell are you doing on here? You're gorgeous. The question is... could you keep up with a 23 year old? ;)

JKind9: Roses are red, violets are blue... nobody has a pretty smile like you ;) and I made it rhyme hahaha x

And finally…

MarkyMark0: Hey, you are lovely. Let's get married?

(Two hours later as I did not reply.)

MarkyMark0: F*** you then.
Me: Wow.
MarkyMark0: Disclaimer: I never wanted to marry you! Seriously, did you actually think that I meant it?! You women are all crazy. You're ruining the world.

(20 mins later.)

MarkyMark0: Aw, you suck! I'm f***ing awesome
Me: And you're saying women are crazy?
MarkyMark0: Apart from my three sisters and niece... you're all batshit crazy.

(One hour later.)

MarkyMark0: And you are crazy anyway. Like I said, you're all to blame for the world's problems. It's true and you know it!!!!

Honestly, you couldn't make this up. And these men wonder why they're single? If I'm honest though, it put the fear into me about my first messages. What if I'm getting it wrong? What do men actually want me to say? I don't even know what I want their first messages to say to me. Just something not creepy or a joke would work! Surely if you're interested, a simple 'hi' is all you need? I'd reply to a 'hi' from a hot normal man!

Chapter Eleven

This is probably why I don't really send first messages. I often just add them as a 'favourite' and hope they contact me. Although so far, this hasn't really worked. And some days I view my 'Your Favourites' folder and wonder whether I was drunk when I added them.

In the middle of all this awfulness was Karl. Sensible Karl. Aged 39, normal, nice, Sensible Karl.

We chatted about how awful online dating is for sometime, and then decided to meet. My first POF date. How exciting! But also terrifying as this was the first time I hadn't been able to check out whether he was normal because he wasn't on Facebook. He lived in Liverpool, which seemed like way too much effort to me (who wanted someone within a 10km radius) but I had a word with myself, as he seemed nice and sensible. We met in a pub half way between where we both lived.

It was an ok date. He didn't really have much to say and his Scouse accent threw me somewhat (I don't know why I hadn't thought that through – I knew he was from Liverpool!) so I had to do most of the chatting. And in the middle of our meal, I cracked a tooth on a crispy roast potato and the pain was horrific! However, I tried to pretend I wasn't a weirdo with weird teeth so carried on like a trooper. (I am a weirdo with weird crumbly teeth.)

The restaurant was closing as it was a Sunday so we walked out to our cars that we happened to park next to each other. We said an awkward goodbye, he gave me a kiss on the cheek and I got in my car. I turned the engine on and I had been listening to Smooth Radio. I must have been listening VERY loudly because suddenly Madonna's *You'll See* was blasting from the car and all Karl would hear were the following lyrics:

All by myself
I don't need anyone at all
I know I'll survive
I know I'll stay alive
All on my own
I don't need anyone this time
It will be mine
No one can take it from me
You'll see.

Totally not cool. He probably thought I was a total bunny boiling maniac.

We exchanged a few texts after our date but it seems Sensible Karl was just too sensible for me.

After him, I had a few messages from Hot Tom who asked me round to sample some wine in his wine cellar. I obviously asked jokingly if he was going to murder me in his cellar and he unnervingly told me he'd given that up. Probably luckily for me, once he realised I wasn't just going to go to his house,

he admitted quite openly that he was just after one thing. Sex.
I presume some girls must say yes? Maybe? Mind blown.

Chapter Twelve

I decided maybe I needed to spread my internet dating wings.

So I joined OkCupid, Zoosk, Happn – the works. Why not? Well, turns out, BECAUSE THEY'RE ALL WEIRD.

So I went back to the paying option and signed up to Match.com. The adverts on the TV were pretty good, I thought. So I paid for one week. It cost me £7.99.

What a waste of money that was. Same people. Same weird messages.

Apart from Welsh James. He looked 'normal' on four of his five photos but the one dodgy one was very dodgy and concerned me and I was convinced that in real life he was going to look like the dodgy one. We chatted and he was funny. He was a banker. And he was Welsh and I bloody love the Welsh! So we exchanged phone numbers and arranged to meet on the Sunday.

Then, in a weird twist of fate, a friend of mine asked if I'd like to go on a date with one of her friends. She sent me a photo and IT WAS A GUY OFF POF WHO I'D BEEN CHATTING TO! But one day he had just stopped chatting, as they generally do.

Anyway – after my friend had a word – he messaged me again, we chatted and he apologized. Then he asked if I wanted to meet him on the very same Sunday as the date with Welsh James. Typical! But as I decided this was fate, I asked Welsh James if we could move the date to one night in the week. He agreed this was actually better for him anyway. Phew! I couldn't go on two dates in one day! That'd be crazy. Right?

So as we got closer to Sunday's date, I was getting quite excited. We'd been texting and he was funny. He was a teacher, had his own place, own car, own family, own friends. Great. On the Sunday itself, I started to get ready and off I went.

A man walked into a bar (this is not the start of one of the jokes I learnt off one of the weirdos) and he walked over to me, smiling. Oh. How very disappointing. I could tell it was him but I didn't recognize him from his photos. Why have photos online when you look totally different in real life? Grr! Anyway, we sat and chatted and he was actually very lovely and very easy to chat to. Sadly though, just not my type. At all.

He made it worse for himself when he told me he genu-inely wants a 1950s type woman who will cook and clean for him whilst he lies on the sofa.

This was my first daytime date and after an hour, I sud-denly thought I didn't know how to end it. All the other dates I'd been on had been evening ones that came to a natural end at the end of the night. But this one had started at 4pm and I was drinking coffee. What was I to do? I couldn't just sit there all afternoon and evening? Hmm.

'Do you want dinner?' he asked. I wasn't quick enough to think of an excuse so I foolishly said yes. I decided what I wanted, went to grab my purse to pay for it at the bar and he told me to put it away as it was on him. It was very nice of him. So I told him what I'd like (hunters chicken) and just before he got up to go to the bar to place the order, he grabbed my face and said, 'Come here you,' AND LITERALLY LICKED MY FACE.

I don't know what happened. Or how it happened. Or how I responded. I just knew that my mouth area, and definitely my chin, was wet.

It still turns my stomach now. Was that a snog? WHAT WAS THAT? Why did he think it was ok to do that? After one hour of meeting me? On a Sunday afternoon? WHO DOES THAT?

We had been sitting underneath a TV screen, which was showing football so it wasn't like there was no one looking in our direction. ALL the men in the pub were facing us. I waited until I thought it had been an ok amount of time, pretending I was totally cool with what had just happened and I managed to subtly wipe my chin dry with a napkin. He came back from the bar. It was weird and awkward, as I'm sure you can imagine. Had I given him the wrong impression? I was just being nice. I tried to change my body language in case that had caused the face lick.

I didn't eat my hunters chicken because I'd suddenly begun feeling sick. But he ate his burger faster than I've ever seen anyone eat anything, ever. Turns out changing my body language had worked though as he said he had to make a move. THANK GOD! So we got up to leave and left. BUT THEN HE DID IT AGAIN! OUTSIDE! IN FULL VIEW OF EVERYONE IN THE PUB!

STOP DOING THAT!

JESUS. Had he not learned? Clearly not. I told him it had been nice to meet him – which was a lie, obviously. I then waited for a few hours before I sent the cop-out text like a 16-year-old saying it had been nice to meet him but I felt no spark. AND STOP LICKING PEOPLE! (I did not say this but I did write that the 'kiss' threw me.) He shall forever be known as The Man Who Licked My Face.

NEXT!

Chapter Thirteen

It should have been Welsh James next. But sadly, it wasn't.

I had texted him asking what day in the week he'd like to meet but he was never to be heard from again. I decided it was karma biting me on the ass. I should never have binned him off in the first place.

So next on my list was speed dating. A single friend of mine asked me if I wanted to join her. Sounded horrendous, but I thought why not? What have I got to lose?

Two hours of my life, face to face with weirdos. That's what.

The most hilarious thing about the speed dating was that I had a very weird, suspicious incident with my finger that day. I woke up and my index finger on my right hand was huge, like I had an allergic reaction of some kind. I couldn't bend it. It was so, so odd. It had NEVER happened to me before. I decided to stop in a pharmacy on my way to work to ask if they could suggest anything. They mainly laughed, agreed it was odd and said to try just taking antihistamines but they didn't work.

I started to wonder. Is there such a thing as 'Tinder Finger'? Had I given myself a repetitive strain injury by swiping too much? It was the finger I used on the app! My next thoughts were how on earth am I (a) going to hide the fact I've got a huge finger whilst speed dating, (b) write notes on the speed daters, and (c) avoid being remembered by the boys on the speed dating as 'the girl with the weird big finger'. This was just SO typical. My mate Sam who I was going with obviously found this hilarious.

Off we went to the bar in Manchester city centre where the speed dating was. I was actually really nervous. The sudden thought of having to meet 15 men was terrifying. At least on-line when they send a creepy message, you can just ignore it. This I could not ignore. For three whole minutes. Which is a VERY long time.

Every time the whistle went, I was relieved the current oddball had to move on but was terrified about the next odd-ball that would arrive at my table.

The first man that came to me was SO nervous that he literally could not talk. He could not get out any words what so ever. It was totally awkward. I basically just ended up talking at him for three minutes whilst he nervously nodded.

There was one man with questions actually written down. Things like, 'What do you do for fun?' WHAT KIND OF QUESTION IS THAT? Next one was, 'What is your favourite food?' NO. No, no, no. Where was that whistle?

There was one man whose name I couldn't pronounce so I decided to ask him as he approached me how to pronounce it. He put his hand up to me and said, 'NO! Ask me ANYTHING else other than that. That is the same question that every single girl has asked me. I am bored of that question.'

Bit harsh I thought! It's just a normal genuine question. It's kind of important to know how to say someone's name. I had to think quickly as he was sat waiting for my next question.

But I had nothing prepared. So I said the first thing that came into my head… which just happened to be the last question that last weirdo asked me: 'What is your favourite food?'

Now, what I hadn't considered was that this man was of a larger size than most and therefore he got very offended and asked if I had only asked him that because he was big. Thankfully, the whistle went.

The next guy asked me straight off if I exercise. Thank god! A normal thing to talk about and something I could probably easily fill three minutes talking about. And I was right, I could! That three minutes flew by.

The whistle went and it was the halfway break. Thank GOD! I needed a wine and a debrief with Sam who I could mainly hear cackling with laughter throughout the first 30 minutes.

But, unfortunately, Mr Fitness decided not to leave my table and wanted to continue talking to me about exercise. The conversation went like this (although when I say conversation, he mainly did the talking because all I said was 'no', 'nope', 'no' in response to his questions…):

'Have you tried protein pancakes?'
'Have you tried protein crisps?'
'Have you tried protein bread?'
'Did you know there's protein hot chocolate?'
'And there's protein porridge. Have you tried that?'

I didn't get my wine or a debrief with Sam but she enjoyed watching my pained but polite facial expressions.

Everything you expect Speed Dating to be, it is – except for the fun bit. All my married friends said, 'I think it sounds fun!' – but the only fun part was being safely back in Sam's car after running from the bar in fear of our safety and laughing the whole way home about the weirdo creepies that we'd just met. It was DRAINING! The great thing however was that there was no one I wanted to write notes about so I kept my 'Tinder Finger' well hid under the table.

Never, ever, ever, ever, EVER again.

Two weeks later I get a text from Sam: 'How about a Singles Night?'

She announced that when she bought the tickets for the Speed Dating she got two free tickets to a singles night. I instantly said no. But she's very persuasive and you really do never know...

So off we went – mainly because we got a free glass of Prosecco on arrival.

Well, that was even weirder than speed dating. It was like a school disco. All the girls sat on one side of the room and all the boys on the other with a massive dance floor in the middle.

Two of the weirdo creepies from Speed Dating two weeks before were there and harassed us about why we hadn't indicated we were interested in them. JEEEEEEZ. I left. I didn't even drink my Prosecco.

I could do better than this. I went to a normal bar, which was full of normal people. My intention was to chat to normal men. But I obviously ended up dancing like a fool with my fave gay best friend instead and drinking way too much gin. But at least it was fun.

Chapter Fourteen

I deleted ALL of the online dating apps from my phone. I'd had enough, I was giving up. I decided I'd just have cats or fish, or something.

But just one day later, I thought, well, you've got to be in it to win it, so I rejoined Tinder and Plenty of Fish. It had become like some weird addiction that I clearly couldn't give up. BUT rejoining meant I had an entire new fresh pool of men because it thought I was starting as a newbie. WIN! And so many more men appeared than first time round!

I matched with a good few of them. One was too good looking to be real and in my true, honest style, I told him so. I accused him of going to Google, typing in 'male model', posting two photos and pretending they were him. I thought it was a serious case of the catfish but how wrong I was! Turned out it was him – he gave me his Facebook name, etc., so I could check him out for real. However, it also turns out looks aren't everything because bless him, he was so damn stupid.

Then along came Rock Climbing Gavin. From his photos, he had pretty damn good arms and we got chatting. I am always amazed when guys reply, as it does seem to be a general rule that they don't like to do messages. Gavin seemed normal and funny; he had a good job and was a rock climber.

He asked if I wanted to go and meet him in a pub on the Friday night but he was going to be with his mates so we both decided it would be weird. He said he might be free on the Saturday but I didn't hear from him till the Sunday – we were still messaging through Tinder having not swapped numbers at this point.

On Monday, (this is starting to sound like a Craig David song), HE GAVE ME HIS NUMBER! Wooo! I figured this would mean we could finally organise a date. So I Whatsapped him – I've learnt that this way, when they reply, hopefully they're stupid enough to have their surname on their profile on Whatsapp which allows me to begin my stalking – and he replied (with his surname). WIN!

So, I typed his name into Facebook – and I gasped out loud. He was a married man with two children! I was so amazed, and outraged, and shocked and puzzled. It blew my mind. His Facebook profile was pretty much an open book and I clicked on his wife – who happened to be holding a gun in her profile photo… WE HAD TWO MUTUAL FRIENDS! It was ridiculous. Why do men do this? How do they think it's ok to do this? It's not like their profiles are hidden on Tinder so anyone can see them. Surely his wife had single friends who could see him?

It was absolutely bonkers. And what's worse is that he continued to message me, thinking I had no idea. But oh boy, I knew all I needed to know and I decided to stop replying.

Chapter Fifteen

That was February, a few days before Valentines in fact. Needless to say I didn't have a date for the big night but I did have a large tin of M&S biscuits to myself instead so all was not lost.

Over the next few months, I continued to dabble with both Tinder and POF and met some, well let's say, interesting chaps.

First, there was Stelios, the Handsome Greek. A banker. He was ridiculous. His English was so broken that it made online chatting hilarious. He told me that too many girls on Tinder were time wasters and that he was not looking for a 'paypal'. I thought at first he was a dodgy bloke after my money but the poor guy meant penpal. He was cheeky and persistent but I did not meet him – imagine how difficult actual talking would have been?

Alfred was also interesting. We matched, which was a bonus but his first message was odd:

Alfred: Unfortunately you look way too gorgeous to even consider asking you for what I am looking for here... but thanks for the like anyway.

WHAT?! It intrigued me so I told him to 'try me'. He lived in Germany but travelled the world for work. He told me that every city he goes to, he likes to take a lady out for dinner and then he likes 'dessert back in his hotel room'. He told me he had decided though that he'd rather have me 'for a main course'. Wow! Madness. He actually seemed quite nice and he was very honest – I imagine some men wouldn't admit to all of that and would just have got me to dinner then expected the rest. I asked him if this approach ever works for him and I was amazed when he said that every night, in every city, he achieves what he's on Tinder for. BONKERS! Men are crazy but clearly so are women. I obviously did not meet him.

And there were a few more I politely ignored:

GavinP6: Hey! Do you spend time at Media City? Your face is familiar. Don't worry not some weird stalker. I live here and always remember the pretty girls I see about.

Clearly he was a big weirdo stalker because I did spend time there. It was pretty terrifying and at times, I wondered if I was being watched or followed home.

Some people were less scary, more cheesy which was just pathetic:

Paulo12: Hello! You're the petrol and I'm your match. Let's make a spark together...

No no, let's not.

Then there were the people who had clearly typed 'good opening lines for online dating' or something into Google so, I would get this message:

> After a rigorously brief overview of your profile I wanted to let you know I have already married and divorced you in my mind. Thanks for all the wonderful imaginary memories… you will always have a special place in my heart.
>
> Your ex-hubby,
> B
>
> P.S. You can keep the dog and I'll keep the house in Hawaii ☺

The first time I got this message, I giggled. The guy wasn't for me, but it made me laugh. Fair play, I thought. So I messaged him to congratulate him on his opening line skills.

A few weeks later though, I got the EXACT SAME MESSAGE from a different man. Gutted. So, so disappointed in the first man! I bet he was SO pleased I'd fallen for something he'd Googled. I asked the second guy where he got it from. His response? 'I wrote it.' Good, a liar from the start then. Excellent.

Chapter Sixteen

So then there was Brett. Another guy I was at uni with. There was always something between us but nothing had ever happened. Either he had a girlfriend or I, momentarily, had a boyfriend. For years we'd stayed in touch and seen each other at weddings or birthday parties.

Just before I moved back to Manchester in 2014, he asked if I was back home for Christmas and if I fancied meeting up. I said yes, instantly. He was a doctor, handsome, funny, and silly. Just my type. We met up in town and went for lunch. It was great. But I couldn't quite work out what it was. Was it a date? Was it just two mates catching up? I had no idea. We then went for drinks afterwards and that went on for a few hours.

Over drinks, he told me how at one wedding seven years before, I'd pretty much put a dagger through his heart because I 'blew him out'. As if! I have zero recollection of this. Anyway, at the end of the evening, he said how nice it was to see me and gave me one of those long and lingering hugs. Then we said goodbye. By then, I was drunk on a tram so I decided to text him, telling him to come and visit me in Cardiff. However, it turned into a weird conversation in which he told me that we were both too soon out of long-term relationships blah, blah, blah. And yet literally one month later, I saw on Facebook that he'd got a new girlfriend. Say whaaaattt?! He'd told me he wasn't ready for a relationship. Clearly, just a load of that bull that boys continually give me.

Whatever.

Fast forward eighteen months on and one morning, I got a new message on Plenty of Fish. I naturally assumed it was a weirdo, especially when I saw what it said:

Phwoarrrr you're well fit. Will you come on a date with me?

It was from Brett. Was I dreaming? Hallucinating? Nope. There he was. I replied asking him WTF his was doing on there. He told me his girlfriend had dumped him out of the blue a few months before so he was trying to find someone new. We moved off the app and went to traditional texting. He said he'd love to take me out for dinner and asked when was I free. I desperately and hopefully told him I was basically free forever and he said he had some things to do, some shifts at the hospital to sort but then he'd definitely get in touch to make a plan. I can only presume he's still sorting things because I never heard back from him. Maybe he's having too much fun with girls from Plenty of Fish?

*****

All of my friends and family ask how dating is going.

My answer generally is, 'It isn't.'

'I'm sure I must know some suitable single men,' everyone says. But no one ever does.

So I was rather surprised when my friends Jude and William told me about their single friend who was a personal trainer. I decided there was no way he'd be interested in me as he's super hot and must spend time with toned attractive girls so I ignored it and forgot about him.

Some time later, I got a notification to say he'd looked at me on LinkedIn. Then he followed me on Twitter, so I followed him back. We started up a conversation about my biceps – I told him I had big plans to get biceps like Madonna and abs like Jessica Ennis – and next thing I know we were speaking on the phone a few times a week. We were also having a daily text chat.

Problem was, he lived in London but he told me he was coming up to Manchester in six weeks with work. So we decided to meet up.

I was so nervous. Getting on so well with someone on the phone was one thing but what if we'd both invested six weeks of chatting and there was no connection? We had accidentally momentarily FaceTimed each other but it was terrible timing. I'd just been to hot yoga and was SO sweaty and he'd been travelling for a few hours and was all hot and flustered. We decided it was a bad idea to see each other for the first time on an accidental FaceTime call so hung up.

I went into town to meet him and instantly we connected. It was like meeting with an old friend who I'd known forever. OMG. Excellent. Maybe this was it? Who needs online dating when you can have recommendations from a friend?

We went for dinner, then drinks and I ended up back in his hotel room. No, not like that, I genuinely went in for an innocent cup of tea whilst I waited for a taxi. But it was ridiculous. I ended up trying to do handstands, which I had not thought through. Going upside down means top falling down! Why

71

had I not thought to tuck myself in? Why was I even in this man's room doing handstands?

Well, there was a reason: I was injured and he was a PT who knows about injuries. Early on in our phone conversations, he suggested I try yoga and even Googled to find me a yoga class near work and one near where I live (could he have been any more perfect?) So I'd been doing yoga for a few weeks before we met. The teacher at one of the places was all about being upside down but I'd been too chicken to try it so that night in his hotel, he was trying to prove to me I could do it. Turned out, I could! Who knew? Ok, so I did collapse the first time round after ignoring his guidance:

'Make sure what ever you do,' he said, 'that you lock your shoulders. Promise me you're going to lock your shoulders.'

I did not lock my shoulders. It was a random silly first date. As my taxi arrived, he asked if I was free the following night because he'd love to see me again.

I ended up seeing him three nights in a row. The third date gave me slight concerns because he was often checking his phone and I noticed he had a lot of text messages off his ex-girlfriend. But I chose to ignore it.

He then went back to London. Boo. Why did he have to live there? How had I met someone who didn't live nearby? Typical.

It was ok though because in our many conversations, he had talked of moving and how much he liked it up north. Hundreds of people survive long distance relationships – not that this was a relationship, it was only three dates! I cautioned myself not to get too carried away and we continued to chat regularly. It was great.

Not long after, he told me he was going to Liverpool for work but he was going to stop by Manchester on his way home to see me. I frantically tidied and cleaned. I also rushed back from town because I stupidly attempted to run a 10k that morning. (That was a huge error and I'm now officially a retired jogger!) He called me, I assumed to say he was lost or outside. But in fact, it was to say that he wasn't going to make it. He told me he'd put my postcode into his satnav and it was going to take him an extra 26 minutes to get home to London if he came to see me and he was tired.

WHAATTTT THE.......?

He'd spent the day watching his ex play football instead. I was gutted, properly gutted. Clearly he wasn't over his ex and wasn't that bothered about me. GAH.

I sent him a text message because I just wanted to know where I stood. I didn't have time to invest in someone who wasn't that bothered. The film *He's Just Not That Into You* was screaming at me.

He called and we chatted and he said he was not over her. If she had appeared at his door and asked him to get back with her, he'd say yes. Great. So I was just some other girl who was taking his mind off her. Standard.

He was very honest so I have to give him that but I decided to cut contact and if he sorted his head and heart out and came back to me at any point then I'd consider him again but for now I had to move on and forget he existed.

Chapter Seventeen

I matched with an attractive man called Steve. He looked fun and silly. Great.

One of his photos was of him playing the trumpet so I sent a message.

Me: Hi Trumpet Playing Steve.
Steve: Hi Nice Dress wearing Shelly.

It was not normally this easy. We chatted and there was good banter, which was great and once the comedy, nonsense, random, chitchat was done, I got down to the boring but important bits of information.

Me: So where you from, trumpet playing Steve?
Steve: LA. I'm here with work at the moment. I play trumpet for Dolly Parton and she's on tour. But she's in Manchester tonight, as am I – obviously.

Wow. How do I meet these people? He asked if I fancied a drink after the show. But that meant having to go out and meet a random man at 11pm, which to me was even more dangerous and weird than meeting a random man at 7pm in daylight.

HOWEVER, he suggested we meet in the pub where my Nan and Grandad had their first night of wedded bliss (even though I don't like to think about what happened there). So maybe this was a sign?! And he was lovely. And he was Dolly Parton's trumpet player. No, no, no. This was silly. I texted my friends to get their opinion. I sent them photos of what he looked like. They told me to go. They told me, 'You only live once,' and that I needed some fun.

Did I go? God, no. I decided it'd be a disaster because we'd OBVIOUSLY fall in love then I'd be heart broken because he lives in LA and travels the world with Bette. So I made up a lame excuse and moved on.

*****

I moved on to more nonsense...

LawroLo: Hey sweetie. I am only here for a few days. Are you interested in having a thrilled night?
Me: Nope.

Then there was 'Jenny'. Yup, a message from a girl.

She claimed that she was 'a bit bored of the weird blokes online and fancied a proper girlie chat'. I'm preeeeety sure that's what friends are for? I reckon it was a man. A dirty, pervy old man who was trying a different tactic to get girls to talk to him, befriend him and then meet him. Terrifying.

The other thing that's terrifying is the fact you don't even need to type a message on POF anymore if you don't want to. You can send an audio message straight into someone's inbox!

As 'David678' from Salford did, in what I presume was his best sexy voice. It's just weird. Really, really, really weird. Why they thought this feature was a good idea I have zero idea.

Next there was Nick. He was very handsome and we matched on Tinder. I'd seen him on there months and months ago and clearly he didn't swipe right for me but had changed his mind. Bonus! His info said he owned a wellness spa, which I decided was another moment of fate and a sign because only a few weeks earlier, my mum and I were looking at his company as we were going to send my pregnant sister there. So I sent a message telling him this. I bet most girls would say the same thing just for something to say but I was serious! He replied. Woop!

As with everyone, the chat began and he seemed to be pretty genuine. We started to chat about yoga (he went EVERY morning). I told him about my new found love for it.

'Where have you been all my life?' he replied.

'Waiting for you?' I said, cheesily.

We chatted for about two weeks and I started to wonder if it was pointless. Chatting is great and fine but if we were never going to meet, I was not after a Tinder chatting friend for life. So I braved it and asked if he fancied meeting up. He agreed!

I instantly panicked though because I'd not been on a date with a guy off the internet since the man who licked my face incident! But I figured I couldn't be afraid of that for life. So I sent him my phone number. His reply was rather odd:

Nick: I may sound crazy but I try to limit SMS to a small circle. I have a crazy system around notifications etc.

Now then, yes you do sound crazy. Firstly, who says SMS nowadays? I bet most of you reading this won't even know what SMS stands for? (Short Message Service or text message.) And what kind of crazy system was he talking about? He definitely sounded crazy but I decided maybe he'd given his number out previously then had found crazy mental girls who stalked him or something. So, for now, I would accept his weirdness.

We planned to meet on the Thursday at 6pm. We decided on the village where we would meet but that was it. No firm plan of where etc. It got to Thursday and I still had not heard from him. I decided that, so far in my awful online dating journey I'd always been the chaser, so this time I did not message him and waited to see what happened.

By 5pm, it was time to leave work and still nothing. The girls in work were gutted and annoyed for me. But hey, that's online dating for you! Then at 5.10pm, my phone goes. It was him! He told me to meet him outside The Met pub in Didsbury at 6pm but that he only had an hour.

This made me a little cross – and the girls in work very cross! They told me that if he was only willing to give me an hour of his time, I should just bin him off. However, I thought I might as well just go because an hour means that the awkward end to a date doesn't happen. I did decide though that I wasn't too bothered so I didn't get changed into the clothes I'd brought with me. I had chipped nails, was wearing my Nike Airs. I hadn't brushed my hair since the morning and I couldn't be bothered to even powder my nose to take the shine off. So off I went. I had a tiny moment in my car of 'what the **** am I doing?' but thought if I don't go, I'll never know and can't moan that I'm single if I'm not willing to try.

Chapter Eighteen

In the car park, I could see a very attractive man sat in the beer garden. He looked like he belonged in a film. A good, thick amount of dark black hair, a great tan and dark eyes. I decided it definitely wasn't him. I mean, it looked a little like him and I know I said he was handsome but not THAT handsome.

I panicked about how I would know it was him. Then I also panicked about how I should greet him. Hug? Kiss? Shake hands? God, I'd forgotten how awful all of this was.

I got out my car, walked through the pub towards the man as he was the only one who was alone. He smiled at me. It WAS him! BOOM! He had recognised me purely from the fact I was limping (still had boring ongoing injuries) which was a little embarrassing and probably not very attractive.

So we only had one hour. GO! What were we going to talk about? Turns out we talked about THE most random things I've ever spoken to a guy about.

One of the first things he told me was that he's not really a fan of wearing shoes. If I'm honest, I thought this was a bonus as I am not a heels/shoes kind of girl. I'm the one who on nights out and at weddings, etc., can be found at the end of the night searching for where I left my shoes hours earlier.

So the chat was great. He was handsome. I made some small errors because I was overwhelmed by his looks – for example I was trying to impress him by telling him I'd recently been 'Stand Up Paddle Boarding' and that I felt restricted in my wetsuit; however, I used the word sophisticated rather than restricted. He laughed. A lot. I couldn't decide if that was good or bad.

Anyway. Very quickly, the hour was up (he actually gave me an hour and twenty minutes) and off we went. I chuckled all the way home about the fact I had made zero effort for a very attractive man and said very stupid things. I decided that since I'm always the one who sends a message afterwards to say, 'Was great to meet you', this time, I wasn't going to. But moments after I got home my Tinder went off.

It was him! Apologising for having to leave saying it was really nice to meet me and that we should do it again! WHO KNEW?!

*****

We chatted more for a few days (on Tinder still) then planned to meet the following week. I suggested a drink/ food/walk. He opted for a walk and asked if I knew of any good walks. Now, if I had lived in Wales, I'd know many but in Manchester, I have no idea, especially for after work walks. The sun was going down at 9.20pm. So, I asked my dad. He suggested a water park/nature reserve in Chorlton.

We met there. You should know that I did totally think about the fact that last time I made zero effort for this guy so the night before our walk, I planned my outfit and left it out so I'd take it with me to work. But I forgot it... so, yet again, I was going to meet him in my scruffs: jeans, vest top and Nike Airs.

We had instant chat again but the waterpark was pretty small and within 20 minutes, we had walked around the entire lake. It was such a beautiful, warm, sunny evening that it was a shame to only spend 20 minutes of it outdoors so we decided to look for more options. There is a canal off the waterpark, and there are many ways you can walk there. So we picked one at random and carried on.

It wasn't until the next day in work that someone pointed out to me how dangerous it is to meet someone I've only met for an hour and go for a walk down a canal with them. Anyway, I'm still alive so clearly he didn't murder me, which is a bonus.

We walked for two and a half hours, just chatting nonsense. But then, when we ended up back at our cars, it got a little awkward. We began making weird small talk. It was odd. He even asked what I keep in the boot of my car, and I showed him. Weird. We'd not needed small talk until now. I couldn't work it out. In the end, after about eight awkward minutes of hovering around my car he said, 'It's been a pleasure again, let's do this again sometime soon'.

I simply said, 'Deffo.'

We had an awkward hug and I got in my car.

Hmm. Why was it weird? I questioned it. Maybe he wasn't right after all. Maybe I just didn't fancy him? I couldn't put my finger on it. Something felt weird. He was a little 'alternative' (I actually want to say hippy/caveman-esque) and he's all about evolution, natural products. He ate paleo (basically like a caveman) and didn't believe in doctors and dentists... all totally bonkers 'out there' stuff. Anyway, I was intrigued and very aware of his beauty but for some reason, I was unsure if I fancied him which made NO sense at all. He was the most handsome man I'd ever seen who wasn't in a film.

We chatted more (STILL on Tinder) and he asked if I wanted to meet for date three. He said if the weather is nice, we should do a little walk followed by a drink. This time we planned to meet at 8pm which meant I could definitely get changed and look nice! I was due at the dentist that day (as well as boring ongoing injuries, I also have dodgy teeth that I promise is NOTHING to do with my love of Haribo!) to have a temporary crown taken off and a new one put on. A simple process, I was told. However when I got there, I had toothache which I thought was normal but I told the dentist. I ended up having emergency root canal treatment at 4.30pm! That meant a numb face, dribbling mess and general unattractiveness. I messaged him to tell him this news. He asked me if I wanted to postpone. I did want to but I also didn't want to.

I had kind of gone off the idea of him. I don't know why but I just had. Oh, did I mention he had no TV? And had no idea who Jessica Ennis or Mo Farrah are? So, I thought I might as well go, rather than draw out chatting to him. If it was going nowhere, I'd rather just be done with it. So I dribbled my way through eating scrambled eggs and went to meet him. One of my mates always used to tell me that by the end of date three, you know if you really like them so I needed to go.

He told me to meet him at the pub where we would go for a drink after the walk. I Googled the name of it and headed there. However, my satnav took me to a pub with a different name. It was in the middle of nowhere with zero 3G and obviously I didn't have his number so I couldn't call him. OMG, I was going to have to stand the poor boy up! What could I do?

I went into the pub I was at and asked where the right pub was. They could tell me it was in a different village about ten minutes away. Great. Hmm. What should I do? Stupid boy not giving me his phone number! I explained the situation and they let me have a wifi password so I could message him. They obviously thought I was totally mental but I didn't care.

Phew. He gave me the correct postcode and I told him I'd be 11 minutes late. When I finally arrived, there he was, outside, looking all lovely. I suddenly didn't know why I was so worried. I clearly did fancy him, I was clearly having a bad day last time I saw him.

He mocked me for being crap at directions, mocked me for looking like I've had a stroke and mocked me for the fact the anaesthetic was so strong that it made one of my contact lenses not work properly so I couldn't really see. I decide mocking is good – isn't it a sign of affection or something?

We walked through some amazing woods by some water that I had no idea was there. It was fun. We got lost, had a laugh. Good times. Then we went to the pub for a drink (sparkling water). It was nice to sit opposite him rather than walk beside him, (i.e. it was good to be able to stare at his face!) He was so ridiculous and random and the things he believed in were TOTALLY bonkers, but I kind of liked it. He was definitely an interesting character.

So, it came to the end of the night and we walk outside the pub and have the very same awkwardness as the week before. But then I suddenly realised why... he kissed me. He was clearly trying to work out if it was ok or something. Jesus, it was ok. Here was a handsome, funny guy who doesn't lick my face but actually kissed me properly. YES! (Although I did feel a little bit like I was 15 kissing a boy outside a pub on a Tuesday night.) He then giddily ran off laughing all the way to his car. I smiled all the way home, obviously having zero idea how to get there.

*****

The next day he messaged me (yes, on Tinder) and said lovely, nice stuff. Win. However, Tinder failed me. It wouldn't let me respond! AGH! If I deleted the app to reset it, Nick would be gone. And I had no contact details for him! AGH! I panicked. I tried to send a message about 17 times. I then panicked that he'd get it 17 times and suddenly think I'd gone from being a normal girl to being one who sends 17 messages.

I waited for a few hours. Still the same. Message failed. AGH!

I turned my phone off and left it off for another few hours.

Oh god, I thought, he's going to think I'm ignoring his lovely message.

AGH.

At 6pm, it finally sent. I apologised in case he got it 17 times and explained that I think Tinder was broken.

Me: Maybe I'll try again to offer you my phone number.
Nick: Great idea Shelly. What's your surname?

I hadn't even realized we'd not crossed the surname path. It was VERY unlike me to not have asked! But I finally had his phone number.

It was nice to have moved communication platforms. However, he chose to text rather than Whatsapp, which in the dating world that I know, is very unusual. But maybe it was a good thing. We planned date four.

Chapter Nineteen

Date four was one week later…

We decided to meet in an area that looked to be halfway from where we both lived that had some kind of green area that we could walk around. So we found a pub in the area and met there. However, when I turned up he was already there, standing outside a boarded up pub. FAIL.

We had both passed something that looked like a park so got back in our cars and drove there instead. It WAS a park! A pretty park! But a pretty, tiny park. This was suddenly becoming our 'thing' – finding the shortest walks ever. We awkwardly walked around the outskirts, which took approximately six minutes. So we decided to walk into the town centre of where we were… which took a further six minutes. This was a disaster. Luckily, we both saw the funny side of it.

So back in our cars we got again and drove to Hale – a really lovely village nearby, which I knew fairly well – so we could go for a drink. Obviously, we ordered sparkling water – it seemed traditional for us now, as this was our third time in a pub without a proper drink. It turned out to be a really lovely evening. Again, sitting in a pub, facing him and chatting about all kinds of nonsense. I really did like him. A lot.

We walked back to our cars where he stopped and kissed me again. It was even better than the first time, probably because it was less awkward. Although, still a little awkward as it was on a road outside someone's house but who cares. A handsome man was kissing me! I asked him when he was next free there and then. Why not? Got to grab these opportunities when they appear!

'Saturday,' he said. That was in like, two days! YESSSS! I had another date with him in only a few days time! This NEVER happened. Date five? I'd managed to get to five dates with a guy? Madness.

So, on the Friday night before the Saturday arrived, I was shopping in the Trafford Centre for a gift for my friend's new baby and I went to look at my phone to see what time it was, and it was switched off. Switched off FOREVER. Yup, my phone had decided to give up.

I did not panic. I could live without my phone, right? I don't need to check Facebook, Twitter and Instagram constantly anyway. And emails can wait. But OMG. OMG. OMG. Date five was planned for the next day at 11am but we hadn't arranged a meeting point! He'd told me to drive to Wilmslow where he lived and call him and he'd come and find me – but how could I do that with no phone? Also, my phone is my satnav and without it, I don't know my way around anywhere. I'm useless!

Ok. No, need to panic. I could get his number off iCloud or something because I DEFINITELY back up my phone all the time. ALL THE TIME. Right? I got home and logged on.

iCloud was obviously down for maintenance work. So it was time to get my thinking cap on. I used my laptop to message my dad on Facebook to see if he had a spare phone.

(Annoyingly, the boy and I weren't friends on Facebook – it took long enough for him to give me his phone number so I thought a friend request was pushing my luck at this stage!) Thankfully, my dad could help, so I went over.

I explained the situation to my step-mum who went into panic mode because she's so desperate for me to get a boyfriend.

'But what will you do?' she said. 'How will you get his number? Oh god Shelly, you knew your phone was dying, why did you leave it until it got this bad?'

Yes, yes, yes. I knew all of this. So Dad ended up lending me his phone. He decided he could do without it for a few days (legend) and he lent me his actual satnav so that I could at least get to Wilmslow for date five. The only issue now was the boy's phone number. I decided it'd all be ok in the morning as iCloud would be back up and running and I'd find his number somehow.

So I went to sleep... panicking.

The following morning I woke up to discover my phone had decided to switch back on! YESSSSSS! It was all going to be ok! Technology was on my side! So I drove as planned and called him as if there had never been a problem at all.

*****

Romantically, he had told me to meet him outside Waitrose. I had offered to pick him up from his house but he said it was easier for me to meet him there so that's what we did. It was another lovely, sunny day. Every date so far had been so sunny. We were so lucky. So, he suggested we go for a walk (also a date tradition as you may have now noticed). I wasn't aware that Wilmslow led to a beautiful forest, which then led to a mill with an amazing waterfall. We walked for about 40 minutes with the usual nonsense chitchat.

Part of the nonsense chitchat was him telling me that he thinks he's dead inside, that he doesn't think he has any emotions but he'd like some. I wasn't really sure where it was going but it was quite the theme for the walk. Then, he suggested we stop and sit on a bench in the sun overlooking the waterfall. Now this WAS romantic. It was ideal! This was an amazing date! He put his arm casually around me and I casually (but cautiously – didn't want to appear TOO keen) leant into him. I had secret inner chuckles going on. This is the kind of stuff I'd dreamt of for years!

Sadly though we were both tight on time as I was going to an afternoon BBQ with friends and he had to go to work, so after a nice long sit, we headed back to the car. I totally didn't want it to end – ever – but hey, hopefully there'd be date six?! It was all ever so rushed back at my car as it had taken us longer than planned to get back. So a quick little peck on the lips and off he went into the distance on his bike. But he did say, 'Right, Miss, see you next time'. NEXT TIME! Woooo!

He'd started calling me 'Miss' on text messages. I liked it. At first I thought it was a little strange, but I'm not a 'babe' kind of girl.

Date six sadly wasn't as soon after as I'd have liked. It was the following Thursday, which meant I actually only had to wait for five days so it was ok, I could deal with that – best I've had in a long time! We had talked about going to the cinema for something different to do. However he then 'joked' about whether I offered candlelit massage at my flat so I panicked, asked EVERY girlfriend I could find what I should reply and they told me to go with it. So I told him I had candles if he could bring the oil… but I then had a further panic and instantly sent another text message saying, 'I live by lots of green, we can go for a walk' so that he didn't think I was a filthbag.

He agreed he'd come to me. OH. MY. GOD. SO many things to consider… My flat must be spotless – first impressions are everything (although I didn't worry about this for date one and how I looked!). Should I offer to cook? Or did I casually have some food in the fridge that I could throw together? Would he stay over? Would I need to shave my legs and 'other areas'? Oh god. Why didn't I just agree with the cinema plan?

Before I knew it, there he was, in my car park. A handsome man coming to visit me! He came in and we had a semi-awkward discussion in my hallway about whether we were going to go for a walk or not. I showed him on a map on my phone where it was and realized I was actually suggesting a six-mile walk which wasn't ideal as it was due to go dark in about an hour's time. So, instead, I offered him a drink (of sparkling water), he took his shoes off (it seems he does actually wear shoes) and came in. I had music on, candles lit… perfect.

He didn't want to eat (luckily I ate a huge bowl of cereal before he arrived to tide me over just in case) so we just sat on my sofa and chatted. It got to 9pm and he told me he had to go. He had a strict bedtime of 9–10pm – his 'window' as he called it. He said that if he's not asleep by 10pm, he's screwed for the night and won't sleep at all. He explained that he doesn't know why, but that's just what happens. But then, he suddenly started kissing me. He hadn't done that all night! Why wait until he announces he's leaving? One thing OBVIOUSLY led to another and it was another hour before he left. I decided it was his own fault but it was a win for me as it meant I had him for another hour!

'See you next time,' he shouted as he left. So that meant I was going to get to date seven? Crazy. I discussed what this meant with my gay best mate James. He told me that as a rule, you stop counting after ten and that it means you are boyfriend and girlfriend.

Texts between us were getting fewer and fewer; I was aware he wasn't much of a phone user so decided it was ok. If I texted him, he'd always reply. And pretty instantly. He just wasn't one for huge text conversations. I had no idea what he was doing day to day, no idea what his weekends involved and he also didn't ask me, but I just went with it. It was different to any guy I'd ever dated before which could only be a good thing.

In the meantime, I had 15 days' holiday left with work. I had discussed this with him and I 'joked' that he should come away with me as he needed a break from his job. He told me he had not had a holiday for three years since he opened the business as it would mean having someone work for him full time to keep it running. So I got the picture that he wasn't going to be free for a holiday anytime soon, especially as he'd only ever been free to see me once a week.

My friend Anna had booked flights to go to California in September to get the last bit of summer sun. I love the sun. She had booked to go alone – like me, she's single with not many options for travel companions. So I decided to go for it, invite myself along and book flights. I was going in three weeks' time! So exciting! However, I was weirdly nervous about telling Nick. I don't know why. I tried to put myself in his shoes and if he had announced he was going to California in three weeks, how would I feel? Honestly, I would have been gutted, and wonder why he hadn't asked me. But I kind of had asked him and if we were having full on daily chats or text conversations I'd maybe have talked about my decision with him. But I just announced on a text that I may have accidentally booked flights to LA. He didn't seem bothered at all. Just replied with 'nice'. So I asked him when he was next free. He said the following Thursday. (He doesn't work Thursdays, which is why he always suggests it as his job means he's tied up until pretty late with clients.)

It seemed that he just presumed he'd come to mine, which was fine by me as it meant I didn't have to go anywhere. I had suggested we go to his but he told me he was 'in between houses' so mine was best. This time, I asked if he wanted food before he arrived but again, he politely declined and said he was going to be a while as he was stuck in work. So he didn't actually turn up until 8.45pm. I was aware his bedtime was 9pm so how was that going to work? Maybe this time he'd planned to stay? I just went with it as I seemed to do nowadays.

So he came in, sat down, had a sparkling water. We chatted about his work and how stressed he was. He asked about California and said he was jealous and can't wait until the day he can go on holiday. He said he had realised that he needed to sort out his life as he was trapped by his job.

At about 10.15pm, he announced he really needed to leave because it was actually already passed his 'window'. But again he started to kiss me and again one thing led to another. I told him he could stay but he said he couldn't. I asked why.

'It's complicated,' he replied. 'It's life.'

I had NO idea what this meant. I presumed it meant that after all this time he had a wife and kids and that's why he'd not offered for me to go to his and why I couldn't pick him up from his house. He then told me he hadn't slept in a bed for years! He said that he slept on the floor on a quilt of crystals. WTF?! I literally had no idea. (Apparently it's infrared and everything.) Odd. So odd. So strange. But I told him this and that I thought he was wonderfully weird. The thing is, when we were together, I felt silly even questioning if he was married, if he was dating anyone else, because he made me feel like I was the only one. I felt so safe and secure (and almost loved) by him. It made me feel like I just needed to trust him and not let past experiences make me suspicious.

*****

I went away to a wedding that weekend. He had asked me to send him a photo of me dressed up ready for the wedding; he'd only really seen me in my 'casual' clothes so I presumed he wanted to check what I looked like in a dress. I was staying with Simone – aka my Rules friend – and she decided we needed a good hour on a photo shoot getting the perfect photo. I think we nailed it. He replied to the photo telling me I looked stunning and to have a good time.

Weddings are pretty awful. Nowadays, I'm the only single person at friends' weddings. We've got to the age where everyone is married already. So everyone feels sorry for me. It's pretty grim. But it means that I get very well looked after, i.e. people constantly making sure my wine glass is full, constantly buying me gin, etc. I guess it's pretty great really! It's just the going back to the hotel room on my own that sucks. And breakfast on my own. That sucks too. I try to avoid breakfast by taking a cereal snack bar to tide me over.

Anyway, Nick was quite active on text the day after the wedding. And somehow I convinced him to come over and see me when I got home. It meant he'd not get to me until 9pm so I thought he'd never do it. But he did! (I told him I had the hangover horn – we'd not really done the sexting thing and actually still didn't – that's as brave as I got.) Hilariously, he texted me saying to leave the door unlocked and to wait in my bedroom.

Now then, I am in no way sexy. No way at all. So I rang Lucy and asked her what to do. I couldn't work out if he was joking or being serious for starters. I'd feel SO silly waiting in my bedroom. Would I wait naked? Lying on my bed? Under the duvet? What? In the end, Lucy and I laughed for so long and discussed options that before I knew it, I saw him drive into my car park. AGH! So it actually determined what happened for me. I answered the door. In my PJs. Not so sexy at all. Although I had quickly opted for a shorts and vest top option. He told me he was disappointed I wasn't naked. I just laughed awkwardly. Anyway, again, he only stayed a few hours – but this time past 11pm! It was getting better! I asked him when I'd see him the following week as I was then going on holiday the following weekend. He told me he was hopefully free Tuesday, Thursday AND Friday! Wow. I told him I felt honoured. This was a big step for him! How exciting! This did actually feel like boyfriend grounds.

So Tuesday came... this was DATE TEN! I'd made it! Exciting! However, he'd told me already on text that he now couldn't do Thursday or Friday so this was going to be the last time I saw him until I was back from my ten-day holiday.

He came over – as he always did – wanting no food and having a sparkling water. It was as lovely as ever. Lots of sofa cuddles and general niceness. We discussed my holiday plans. He asked what I was going to miss. I couldn't decide if this was a trap and he was hoping I'd say him. I decided NOT to say it because during one of our many discussions about how he's 'dead inside', he'd told me he doesn't miss people so I knew he wouldn't say it back. So I kind of turned it around and told him what I was looking forward to instead. He told me about more work stresses and how he really did need to change everything about his life. He told me more and more each week. Like he was getting more comfortable with me. LIKE HE WAS MY BOYFRIEND.

The time came for him to leave. I asked him not to. Told him to stay, to try sleeping comfortably in a bed. He told me he wouldn't but he promised next time he would. He left telling me to have a great holiday and he was looking forward to seeing my white bits on my return.

After he'd gone, I thought about it and thought, do you know what? I will actually miss him. So I decided I'd just tell him. So I texted and said that even though I know he won't miss me, I will actually miss him and that I'd bring back a perfect avocado for him. He replied, 'I will look forward to it.'

A few days before I went, I was out for dinner with Natalie, the one who I went to Kos with earlier in the year. She convinced me that after ten dates, it was more than normal to send him a friend request on Facebook. So I did. I pressed 'friend request' then felt sick. I put my phone away and decided to try not to become obsessed with opening Facebook to see if he'd accepted.

Chapter Twenty

I decided to clear out my phone so that I had enough space for as many sunset photos as I needed to take whilst on holiday so I started deleting some apps. I realised that Tinder was still on my phone but I hadn't opened it since the point he finally gave me my phone number. To close your account, you have to open the app and go to your profile and 'delete account'. Whilst I was there, I noticed I had some new matches waiting for me that must have been there for weeks. I also decided to have a quick look at Nick as he was still in my 'matches' list. I was nearly sick. His profile said 'active one hour ago'. What did this mean? Maybe he had gone on for the same reason? Or maybe he had a notification to say he had a new match so he was just intrigued? What did I do? Maybe I was right, maybe he WAS dating different people every night and that's why he was never free. Maybe he did one-hour dates with them like he did with me on our first one as that'd mean he'd be free about 8pm to see me? Oh god. This is not what I need. What do I do? I decided to delete my account and the app as I'd only become obsessed with checking if he'd been online. I'd go on holiday, have a great time and deal with it on my return.

So off I went. For ten days. The best ten days ever. California rocks. It really does. Chilling on beaches, doing yoga at sunset, eating amazing salads with avocado, ice cold beers... general amazingness.

However, Nick didn't ever text me. Didn't check I was there ok. If I was having a nice time. The things I'd hope for after ten dates... so I sent him a text after a few days just to say hi. He replied but a short reply. I'd wait a few more days to see if he was interested in seeing if I was ok. Nothing. He also hadn't accepted my friend request. Odd. Why? Why would you not? Was there something he didn't want me to see? Was he actually married (yes, that popped back into my head) or maybe he was just not a big Facebook user? I'd obviously stalked him on Twitter and could tell he was not really a big Twitter user so maybe it was just that. Yes. I also decide that he was very much all about 'the now' and being mindful so that he was leaving me alone on holiday to have a good time and not have to worry about messaging him.

Two days before I was due to fly home I decided to text him. I told him I didn't want to come home but I had to so I hoped he could tell me he was free to see me and make me happy about it. He replied to ask when I was due back – why would he not have this imprinted in his head and marked in his diary? I told him Thursday. He replied to tell me there was a 45 per cent chance he'd be free to see me on the Friday or it'd be the following week. Really? A 45 per cent chance! This didn't sound like a man who's too bothered to see me. Maybe he really WAS dead inside? And he really didn't miss people? I replied to say that my tan would have washed away by the following week.

So I landed on the Thursday. He wasn't at the airport with a bunch of flowers and a huge balloon waiting to greet me

– which is one of my many life goals. Shame. In fact he didn't message to see if I was back safe. Not until the Friday. When he told me he was actually free. YEY. Ok, I thought, now I'm back, life will be back to normal, he'll have sorted his life out and we will now become boyfriend and girlfriend.

He came over at 8pm. It was really great to see him. Again he made me feel like I'm very important to him. No one had hugged me and cuddled me and held me how he did, for a very long time. He asked loads about my holiday which was nice then asked how my jet lag was. It was pretty bad. He asked if I wanted to go to bed… and he'd join me! He was going to stay and keep to his promise of 'next time'! Having him in my bed all night was lush. He was so cuddly and touchy feely. It was great. I just couldn't sleep. Stupid jet lag. And I think I was freaked out that there was a boy in my bed… I don't sleep well with people in bed with me which I'm aware could be a problem but I'm willing to try and get over it. He did, however, have to set an alarm for 6.15am as he had to get up for work. But this was ok. This was PROGRESS!

I texted him a few hours later to say how much I enjoyed having him with me, he replied to say he enjoyed it too, but then I didn't hear from him until Monday. I'm aware Saturday to Monday isn't THAT long a time but I want MORE! And I only got a text because I sent him one. It's ok, I thought, he wont be able to stay away; his next text will surely ask when he can see me next… but no. Just the one text that day. So I had a huge word with myself: what was I doing? He clearly really wasn't that bothered. I decided I had to say something, but face to face so I could judge the real reaction. I texted him on Tuesday asking when he was next free to see me.

'How is Friday?' he replied. Friday? So a whole week since I last saw him? Ok. Fine. I agreed but made an agreement with myself that I must ask him what was going on.

I then didn't hear from him until the Friday and that was to tell me he would be with me hopefully between 8 and 9pm. That's surely the end of the night, I thought? What was he doing until then? And he had to be asleep by 10pm so I'd only get to see him for an hour? I asked if it meant I got to have him on Saturday as well... he replied to say sadly not, only until 6am again.

This wasn't normal. He wasn't normal. I just wanted normal. Why couldn't I find normal?

I had a glass of wine before his arrival for some Dutch courage. I WOULD be brave enough to say something.

He turned up, smelling and looking as handsome as ever. Gave me a kiss and I went all weak. How did he do this to me? He came in, sat down, we chatted, we cuddled. He told me things about his life. Told me how he has an urge to run away. How he had an email written to his parents telling them he'd gone and not to try to find him but that he was ok and he just needed some time out. He had it written and ready just in case he got to the running point. I asked him if he'd written me an email. He just laughed and said I'd have to wait and see. This man is a mess, I thought. That sort of thought is not right. I couldn't risk a life with someone who could just run away at any point. He was broken. But I didn't know why. He just held me tight and fell asleep. I lay on the sofa terrified as I liked him a lot and him being with me felt so right... but so wrong. I managed to wake him and got him to bed. As I watched him get into my bed I thought, god he's handsome. DAMN HIM for being messed up. Again, it was SO nice to have him in my bed, holding me all night and I actually managed to sleep.

His alarm went off at 6am. It made him hug me harder. Like he didn't want to go. He got up, got dressed but then came back to me and hugged me more. It made me sad, it was like he knew he wasn't going to hug me like that ever again. Maybe he WAS about to run away and I'd never see him again? He told me to stay in bed, gave me a kiss and said, 'see you next time,' as he always did.

I lay awake. Wondering. Trying to deny that this wasn't weird. And that all would be ok. His business was just in a mess. Once it was all sorted, he'd be sorted and we would live happily ever after. But then I remembered I was 34. I wanted a 'normal' relationship.

So I sent him a text:

Me: Morning ☺ I need to be honest with you... again I loved having you over last night, but I want it to happen more, I want to see you more. I went online to find someone to have a relationship with, to do stuff on weekends, to hang out on week nights, to go away with. And I found you... 'wonderfully weird, dead inside Nick'... Every time I see you, I get more hooked on you so I'd rather know now if you don't want the same as me. I know your life is crazy right now but you also must have gone online for a reason. Sorry this is on text, I would rather talk in person but I just enjoy your company when I do actually get to see you. So if you're free at any point this weekend to chat/see me, let me know xxxx

I pressed send and felt sick. I knew what the response was going to be. I just had to sit and wait for it.

It took him two hours:

Nick: Afternoon Miss. Of course I understand.

Unfortunately my life is going to be crazy for the next 8 months at least so I can't give you what you want. And even after then, I'm not sure what I want from life. Happy to talk though but due to my stupid life decisions I wont be free to meet until next week.

I knew it. Gutted. Absolutely typical. But I had so many questions. So I asked when he was free. He told me Tuesday.

Why did this keep happening to me? Was it something I'm doing? I couldn't work it out! Maybe I was purposely going for the unavailable ones?

I called Natalie. She was going through a similar thing with a girl. We decided to meet for a 'crying date' and a walk. As she pointed out, at least we had each other and were going through similar things. But also, as she pointed out, at least I wasn't gay as the gay world really is so much worse! I decided it was probably for the best that I cut my losses as I wanted someone who would at least enjoy one glass of wine with me on the weekend, and enjoy eating a large bag of peanut M&Ms with me (after so many dates, I realised I'd never seen him eat anything! He was a 'paleo' eater which basically meant he was annoyingly healthy) and I wanted someone who would accept my Facebook friend request!

So after I noted down all the pros and the cons and had a nice long walk, I decided it was going to be ok. I had everything noted in my head that I wanted to ask him. Mainly, WHY ARE YOU STILL ON TINDER?

*****

Tuesday came. I presumed he was going to come to mine as that seemed to be what happened now. However, I texted him asking what time he was free. He replied telling me to meet him in the pub where we had the date where I got lost. And to meet him at 8.45pm. I tried not to get angry at the 8.45pm bit and just go with it.

I got there super early. I also made more effort than I did on date one. I wore eyeliner, I repainted my chipped nails. I put nice clothes on. I even straightened my hair. I think I was trying to do an 'in your face, look what you're going to lose'.

He appeared bang on time. Bought me and himself a sparkling water and we went and sat in a nice corner next to the cosy fire. I'd say the perfect place for a perfect date. We initially chatted about where his disaster life was up to with his business, etc., then he said, 'Right, so what's all this then? You want to marry me and have children with me?'

Apart from the fact the answer was actually yes, I said 'NO! That isn't what I said!'

He laughed and said he was joking. We had a very open and honest chat. He said he was jealous that I knew what I want from life. He wanted to get to that point but didn't know how. How did I know that I would like to get married and have kids? I have no idea! And I don't know when I got to the point of knowing this! He still wanted to run away (to Mexico and grow a moustache!) but he knew that wouldn't solve anything.

He asked what I was going to do – was I going to go back online to continue with my search? What he didn't know was that on Saturday after my walk with Natalie I decided to brave it and re-open Tinder. And I saw him. There he was. Handsome Nick. Online one hour ago and 6km away from me. (Like a huge loser, I swiped right for yes to him and still to this day never got re-matched with him meaning he saw me and swiped left.) WHY WERE YOU ON TINDER THE WHOLE TIME WE DATED? That wanted to come out of my mouth so badly… but then randomly he told me I have nothing to worry about as all the girls on there are mental. And without me even having to ask him, he got out his phone and opened it up! And showed me girls on there. Showed me his matches. I couldn't believe he was openly doing this.

I said, 'so you've carried on with Tinder the whole time you've been dating me?' Luckily it came out calmly and like I didn't already know.

'Yes. I don't really know why.'

I asked if he'd met anyone since meeting me.

'God no, don't be ridiculous, I don't even have time to see you, never mind anyone else. I don't even have time to chat to girls on here. I've just got into the habit of opening it and looking and seeing that my life is actually ok in comparison to most of the weirdos on there.'

The girls on there were gross and weird and clearly desperate. So odd to see it from a man's perspective. I saw the messages they sent to him. I didn't know why I'd been worrying about what was the right opening line as evidently other girls didn't think about it. I asked what he thought was going on between us and why he was on Tinder if he a) didn't want a relationship and b) didn't want casual sex. What was the point? He said he originally went on as someone told him about it and the concept blew his mind. Fascinated him.

Including me, he'd been on three dates. First two were weird and needy. I asked him why he continued to see me if he knew it wasn't what he wanted. He said he was being a typical man and not considering the full situation. He was enjoying my company and spending time with someone who made him forget about his stupid messed up complicated (for no reason) life. Said he was drawn to me and after meeting me once felt like he needed to see me again, and again and again (14 times).

We chatted about online dates that we'd been on. Somehow in all these months of dating and chatting nonsense we'd never discussed dates or exes. I shared my stories and he could not believe what I was telling him was the truth. But it made him laugh. And he told me I was making him feel semi-normal. I informed him he is semi-normal (wonderfully weird to be precise) which is why I was clinging on for dear life – and the fact he was beautiful with good teeth.

I decided to ask him for feedback. Why not? He laughed (thankfully). I asked him from a bloke's perspective if I text too much, say the wrong thing, if I'm good on dates, etc. This is all vital important information! But his answer was, 'Don't change anything. You are perfect the way you are. Any guy would be mad not to snap you up.'

He said one thing, though: 'you need to become more of a bitch'. However he instantly took it back. And said, 'No, not a bitch, stay exactly how you are but stop letting guys walk all over you. You deserve more. I didn't realise I was taking you for granted until you've pointed it out to me. Who thinks it's ok to tell a girl you're free for two hours a week but only on a Thursday?'

I told him that he once let me see him for two hours on a Saturday which at that point he butted in and said, 'There you go again, making excuses for me. Stop being so nice, stop letting people off for being crap. You deserve more.'

It was weird hearing this from him.

We discussed many things including other ways I can find a man as he believes the internet dating apps are full of messed up men like himself. One of his suggestions was for me to get an allotment as I like planting bulbs in pots on my balcony. I pointed out I'd like a boyfriend around the same age as me, not a 60-year-old man. He said he couldn't believe he was trying to help me find someone else when clearly we could be together.

The odd thing was, though, I wasn't sad. Not at any point. I weirdly never really felt like he was real. He was almost too perfect on the outside. I often felt like I was watching a film but featuring myself. He just looked too perfect. Perfect hair, perfect teeth, a bloody lovely face, perfect body, perfect muscles. He even has bloody perfect feet. So it was almost like none of what had happened was real. Like it was all a big fantasy in my head. Lots of my friends joked that they didn't think he was real as he'd been in my life for so many months but no one had ever had a glimpse of him. It's odd knowing someone so well, however no one else you know has ever met him.

As we were saying our goodbyes, we were standing outside the pub and he said, 'Well, this is weird'. I thought he meant because we'd probably never see each other again. However, he said, 'This is the very spot where we had our first kiss'. Now, for someone who is 'dead inside' this isn't a very 'non-emotional' thing to say. I told him I hadn't even thought about it. Which I hadn't. So he kissed me and said, 'It's been a pleasure,' and gave me one of his hugs that made me feel like he never wanted to let go. And vice versa. Then he ran off into the distance to his car.

I drove home smiling. What was wrong with me? I'd just said goodbye to the most handsome guy I'd ever met and I was smiling? He'd made me laugh and been so honest that it just made me smile thinking about it all. The ridiculousness of it all.

The next morning I got a text:

Nick: Morning. Thank you for being so honest and genuine. If I ever do run away to Mexico, I promise I won't leave without leaving you a coded message. Enjoy the world of Internet dating, Miss. It's been a pleasure.

Ok. So then I cried. A lot. I had been ok! All was ok!
Gutted.
WHY CAN'T YOU JUST BE NORMAL AND KNOW
WHAT YOU WANT?
Stupid stupid stupid stupid stupid man.
I waited to calm down and compose myself and gave my-self time to think about a reply.

Me: Morning. Thanks for the text. I do think it's a shame as everything feels so natural and 'normal' with you. But I totally understand and appreciate your honesty. Keep being wonderfully weird and dead inside if that's who you really are. And if you ever get a few hours and fancy a walk, a sparkling water and a chat about absolute nonsense, you know where I am. Take care Mr Nick xxx

Gutted. Oh well. It obviously wasn't meant to be. Or was a massive case of wrong place, wrong time.

I had to forget he existed. It was all a big dream. A pretend film. Yes.

So. Tinder. Swiping. Again. Forgot how much it hurt my hand!

It had changed. I don't like change.

Chapter Twenty-One

Tinder's main change was that you had the option to swipe left for no and right for yes like before… but now you could swipe UP to 'Superlike' someone. Now, this seemed way too keen for my liking. You would get notifications if you'd not logged on for a while saying, 'You've got Superlikes waiting for you!' Such a tease… and ALWAYS a disappointment. THE weirdest of weird people are the ones who use that Superlike button. Just odd. What a bizarre new added extra feature!

I matched with a man. Ian. He was handsome!! YES! Ok. Maybe I had been panicking for nothing. We got chatting. He seemed normal. Police officer. Talked about his shifts. I talked about my job. All very normal. After a few hours of on and off banter he suggested I Whatsapp him and gave me his number. I went for it. Why not. Let's get this moving.

I simply sent a 'Hi'. Then while I waited for a reply, I looked at his Whatsapp profile picture. It was a photo of a guy doing a Tough Mudder event. So he was covered in mud. Looked like it could be Ian but he did look a tiiiiiny bit different but maybe it was just that he was just covered in mud.

He replied. 'Sorry I think you have the wrong number'.

However my Whatsapp says message from Sean. Not Ian.

I re-opened Tinder and sent Ian a message telling him he gave me the wrong number. He insisted he didn't. So I asked why he replied to my Whatsapp with what he did. He said it was a 'joke'. Hmm. So I went back to Whatsapp. 'Hi,' I typed again. I got a reply:

Ian/Sean: Yeah we did that, I don't know who you are.
Me: You gave me your number on Tinder.
Ian/Sean: I did what?? I'm not on Tinder! Are you winding me up?
Me: Are YOU winding ME up?
Ian/Sean: Not at all.
Me: I literally have no idea what is going on.
Ian/Sean: So someone on Tinder has given you my number claiming it's theirs?
Me: Yes.
Ian/Sean: Defo got the right number?

I went back to Tinder and told Ian he was clearly having a fun evening giving out random phone numbers. And I congratulated him.

He continued to insist it was his number. What a complete mentalist. Told me I must have typed it in wrong. And gave me the same number again. I told him this was very funny but I had better things to do. He asked why I was being weird as I seemed so normal.

In the mean time Sean over on Whatsapp is still messaging...

Ian/Sean: Is there a photo?

I printed the screen and sent it to whoever it is I was talking to. I was convinced at this point that it was two mates sitting in a pub having a right laugh giving out each other's phone numbers to girls to confuse them.

Ian/Sean: I can assure you that this is my number, I am called Sean and that's not me in the photo!
Me: Ok sorry to bother you.
Ian/Sean: No it's fine! I want to know who is giving my number out.

I didn't reply. I didn't have time for this nonsense! Idiots.
I'd forgotten about the knobs on this stupid app!
I then matched with Richard.
Again. Looked 'normal'. We chatted for a few days. Ok. Normal. (Normal scares me nowadays!) Told him how much I hated Tinder as it's full of nutters. After a few days of general chitchat I got a message that said,

Just in case you get the sudden urge to delete Tinder in a moment of hating it, I'd like to give you my number as you seem pretty cool xx

Then gave me his number. So, off I go. Over to Whatsapp. (This pattern is getting so boring!)
Luckily his profile photo was the same as on Whatsapp which was a bonus. Again we chatted for a few days. Thank god. All very nice and very normal. I decided it's because he's 36.
I did the usual of sending his photo over to my mates to ask what they thought. All agreed he looked nice and normal. Then one morning he messaged me at 8am a totally normal

message asking what my day had in store. I replied with an equally normally message... which he never replied to.

This was getting SO tiring. I thought I should send him another message. But I had to keep remembering Nick's feedback. I wouldn't let guys take the piss. So I didn't send another message. If he was really interested he'd realise he'd not replied and I'd get a message in a few days. Right?

Ok, so he clearly wasn't that interested. WHAT HAPPENED THERE? Why just stop suddenly?

I'm not sure I'll ever understand men. Or Tinder.

*****

Then there was Tinder Chris. 'It's a match!'

I sent the first message. Why not? He looked potentially 'normal'.

'Nice flower and handkerchief' was the opening line I went for. Pressed send and forgot about it. Most guys don't reply. I presume they use it in a similar way to Nick who just used it out of habit, got a match, had a little ego boost celebration then carried on swiping.

Two hours later... 'Chris sent you a new message.'

Chris: Why thank you. Sartorial elegance never goes astray. You have an excellent face, btw x

Oh. He replied. With a nice reply. How unusual. But 'hahaha thank you' is all I could think to say. Why I felt the need to use the 'hahaha' I have no idea.

Chris: I mean it. You're lovely. I know this is hideously superficial x

Me: Tinder is awful, I hate it! But thanks. You're actually really familiar (without that sounding cheesy!) where are you from?

Chris: Hmm Tinder has made me fear for humanity. I live in Didsbury. You? x

Me: Haha don't even get me started!! I live in Sale. What do you do?

Chris: I'm a musician. I play the cello in symphony orchestras. You?

Me: Ooh nice! I produce radio stuff.

Chris: At the BBC? I work there sometimes. Going to Germany with them on Monday.

Me: No, I work in commercial radio. How long you going for? What you doing there?

This is where I expected him to tell me he would be moving there forever and this was a huge waste of time. But no. He was just touring with the Royal Philharmonic Orchestra. As you do.

Ok. He really did seem normal.

We chatted some more.

Chris: Are you still going to be on here in three weeks time when I get back?

Me: I imagine so.

Chris: Well this is good. You seem really nice and really do have an excellent face x

Me: Unless I get Tinder rage and delete it as I often do, I'll be here.

Chris: Hmm likewise. Are we ready to Whatsapp? I fully appreciate this is where I find out you're a 26st lorry driver from Hull who lives with his mum.

Me: Hahahahaha.

(Note to self: I must stop using hahaha's so often.)

Then I did something crazy. I gave him my number. It's usually the other way round.

And there we go. Off into this Tinder pattern of 'moving to Whatsapp'.

Oh and I should tell you at this point that I've upgraded his name to Cello Chris rather than Tinder Chris. Also, how is this the second professional musician I've met on there? Why don't I meet anyone who has a nine-to-five office job?

We decided that on his return from his three-week jaunt in Germany, we would meet for cake. And I looked forward to it.

*****

In the meantime, I continued with my 'search'. I decided to go back to OkCupid and POF. My cousin somehow went on OkCupid having never online dated ever, went on one date... and was now into month five with him. How did this happen? Why didn't this happen to me? So it made me think I should give it another go.

OMG. Within 24 minutes of being on there, I wanted to come back off it instantly.

I mean, they're weird on Tinder, but they were REALLY weird on OkCupid. I feel once again I should share with you some messages as you really couldn't make this nonsense up.

TeddyTez: Are you single and looking for a boyfriend? Do you like my pictures? My number is 07********. I wouldn't ever cheat on you because I'm not like that. I am friendly and kind and helpful and trustworthy and responsible and a respectful man. Am I your type to date at all? I live in Cheshire. Where do you live? What is your name? Are you on Facebook? You are hot and sexy and cute. Would you date a 33-year-old man? Do you like men with or without moustaches? How about a beard? Do you have kids at all if you don't mind me asking?

WOW. Intense. I obviously didn't reply.
However, he did anyway. Three hours later.

TeddyTez: What do you think of me? Am I your type to date at all? Yes or no?

Erm. Get the message from my lack of reply… Or don't? 15 minutes later…

TeddyTez: What is your name? Do you fancy me? Yes or no????

AGH! Terrifying.
Then incoming…

MikeJ: Hi. Do you like boats?

Now my friends thought this was hilarious and told me I should reply. He was funny looking. I didn't want to. Pointless. But for them, I took one for the team…

Me: Yes, I like boats. Why?
MikeJ: Because you should get in your boat and sail your way into my heart. Sorry for the cheese. Lol.

Hmm. Yup. REALLY pleased I replied. Then…

HotHarry: Hey… OMG… how pretty are you!!! Anyway, you need to message me back because in my opinion, every girl needs to date a Chinese guy!!! Intrigued?! Come find out why!! Lol.

Erm… no thanks. There was nothing 'hot' about him.

Chapter Twenty-Two

❧ ─ ♥ ─ ❧

There was this one guy on there who looked cute. I looked at him. What a shame. He was 26. Now I know 'age is just a number' as SO many old perverts online message me to tell me this often, but I just can't do it. I know what I want and what I don't want, and I don't want someone who hasn't yet celebrated their 30th birthday.

I may be making a mistake, I thought. I may be ageist. So shoot me. I make my own rules.

The next day, I got a message off said 26-year-old. Who said:

Boota45: Boooooo there's nothing worse than a cute girl looking at your profile but getting no message off them. How to knock my ego.

I totally know what he meant. You get a notification to tell you when someone has looked at you. And there really is nothing worse than thinking, 'oh, that hot man clearly isn't interested in me... what is wrong with me?' so I decided to reply. Now, you may know by now that I don't waste my time replying to pointless guys but I felt he seemed nice and I'd explain.

> **Me:** You seem lovely and are an attractive guy, and I know 26 isn't a massive distance from 34, but I just don't date guys that age. Sorry xx
> **Boota45:** WHAT? I'm 29!? Does it say I'm 26?!

Here we go. This happens often too. There are some actual kids on there who put their age as older so that you fall for the trap, open their profile and read it says, 'I'm actually only 18 but am interested in older women'.

So I questioned him. He told me the photos were also old of him and were from when he was about 26. He said:

> **Boota45:** Imagine my face but with more facial hair. What do you really look like?

Erm. Call me weird but I look like my photos. Because why wouldn't you put up-to-date photos on?

ANYWAY. We got chatting. He actually seemed nice. He was funny. While I talked to him, I continued to get awful weird perverted messages so I told him I need to close the app as I couldn't stand it any longer. So we swapped phone numbers. My first rule was he had to prove his age which he did by taking a photo of his driving licence and sending it to me. Then I asked to see what he looked like 'nowadays'. He firstly sent me a comedy photo of some guy off the internet covered in bacon as he'd been saying how much he needed a bacon sandwich. Funny. Then he sent an actual photo of him. Ok, yes, he's still cute. But with facial hair. More than I usually like but I can see he has a good face underneath so I'm sure I can convince him to trim it before our wedding. Yes. All's ok.

He asks for a photo of me. Shock horror, I LOOK THE SAME AS MY ONLINE PROFILE. Idiot.

Then. Out of nowhere, he asks me:

Boota45: How do you feel about hairy chests?

I mean. If I had a choice and could design a man, he wouldn't have a hairy chest. But they exist. And I can deal with it. Fine. So I say, 'They're ok, why?'

I then get a photo of a VERY hairy chest. Like, VERY. But not just that. No no. FOR SOME REASON (yes, I'm shouting) for SOME REASON he decided to GIVE ME A PUBE SHOT TOO! Who does that? WHO? And WHYYYYYY?

I decided that much like the photo of the man covered in bacon, it MUST be a joke.

Me: What did you Google to find that? Very very hairy man?
Boota45: No... that really genuinely is me. Is it that bad?

THAT BAD? It's gross. Why would you send me that? WAS HE TRYING TO BE SEXY?

Anyway. This boy is now referred to as 'The Bear' for obvious reasons. It's actually a shame as he really did seem nice. And I probably would have met him for a drink. However, knowing what is going on under those clothes, no thanks. So it got a little awks. I decided I'd have to wean him off me somehow. It wasn't easy. He was ever so keen. If I didn't reply to a text for 20 mins, I'd get another three. I can now see why guys get angry when girls do this. CALM DOWN! So I told him a little lie. Which is awful, I know. But I could hardly be honest and say 'you need a shave, love', could I? And really, he still was breaking my rule of no one under the age of 30. So I said that chatting to him had made me realise that I wasn't ready to date and that I didn't want to lead him on. But that I wish him luck (with his extreme hair) on his dating quest. Bless him. He was so lovely. And he still texts me now asking for advice on dating and what he should do in certain situations with girls. My honest answer should just be 'get rid of the hair on your face, trim the hair on your chest... and as for everywhere else – BE GONE! And you'll fall in love.'

*****

Meanwhile over on Plenty of Fish...

Andiiiiii: I love cake too! Do you really speak Arabic?

What a random thing to say! What is WRONG with these people? (Ah. You have to choose your first language from a drop down on languages on a list. Arabic is the top one. I clearly hadn't read it properly and it automatically saved as that. So maybe I was the idiot. In this ONE instance)

Then there was RobCH4. Absolutely stunning. Obviously told me he was personal trainer.

We got chatting. He confessed he's just after sex. Fine. I'm not which I'm honest about. But I think he decided to make me a challenge. Try and change my mind.

He told me he's actually also a 'Butler in the Buff' on the weekends and that he gets a lot of 'action' at the parties. Told me SO much stuff about how it works, the girls, told me I could ask him anything about it. I think he thought it was a huge turn on, but sadly it was a huge turn off. Such a shame. Such great arms.

There are so, so many weird people out there. I started to miss my weekly meeting with 'wonderfully weird Nick'. So I texted him to see how he was. He was ok. His life was the same. Not much change. APART FROM THAT HE WAS CLOSING THE BUSINESS! That surely meant he'd be free? And lost and have time to think... and realise he couldn't live life without me?! I tried not to get carried away. I remembered he'd not messaged me first to tell me this. I was the instigator. I asked if he fancied a catch up and a sparkling water. He did. He really did. But only if I was ok with it, apparently. So I met him, hoping he'd gotten ugly. And fat. But no. Still as handsome as ever. Bugger. Ok. I could deal with this. We could just be friends. We chatted. It was SO lovely to see him. He seemed comfortable with me. And I was ever so comfortable with him. But that was it. We had our time and said our goodbyes.

*****

Cello Chris was back. He texted a few times whilst in Germany. Nothing major, but kept himself in the 'game'. We re-started the chat about meeting for cake. He actually, I think, was the most normal I'd chatted to so far!

Until... I wake up one morning. I'd received a message from him at 4.45am:

Chris: As if I've got cocking jet lag and am bang awake at 4am after sleeping for 12 hours 8-8 last night?! Anyway. I feel like I need to be honest. I'm not really sure why but I don't feel I'm in a 'datey' kind of place right now. I genuinely can't put my finger on why, not been on one since March and as much as I should get back on the horse, I somehow can't face it at the moment. I'm not sure if it's currently due to the fact that I've recently had to give my ex a load of money/ sever all ties, but I really can't face it at the moment. I needed to tell you this as you seem utterly lovely. xx

Oh… Good. Great. Perfect. Perfect perfect perfect. Knew this was another 'too good to be true' scenario.

However, at least he had said it now rather than three months down the line. So I replied:

Me: Morning. Don't worry. Dating is hard and actually sucks. I hate it! And Tinder! I'm not a big dater myself so I totally get it. Thanks for being honest. It's best you're in the right place for it. I think you seem very lovely yourself so all of this makes sense as I genuinely don't think online dating is for 'normal' and nice people, so this just proves to me that I was right in thinking you were nice and normal! I'm pleased I got it right ☺. Anyway, I hope your jet lag doesn't last too long. If you get to a point where you fancy trying a piece of cake with a stranger then we can pretend we are old school friends and it's not a date, then just let me know xx

Chris: Awww YOU!! Thanks! I can always do cake with a stranger! I can assure you though I have my moments of vintage bellendry though. Thankfully they are becoming more infrequent these days. But I try and shield nice people from them... cake in West Didsbury soon for sure please. Working Saturday then back at my folks Sunday. But next weekend maybe xx

Woah woah woah. It was him who said he didn't want to do this. And within six minutes he'd changed his mind? Because I said we could pretend to be school friends? Madness. Men are mad. Bonkers.

Because I'm, like, well cool and well popular, I couldn't do the following weekend as I had booked a last minute weekend away to Copenhagen with some girlie mates and I couldn't do the weekend after as I was going on a yoga retreat in the Lakes. So IN YOUR FACE, Mr 'I can't do this right now. Well actually yes I can'.

We got a 'date' in our diaries to meet the following Sunday. I was convinced he'd bail. He went a little quiet on text but then he did play the cello for various orchestras so I guessed he was busy...

The day before we were due to meet, I got a Facebook notification, telling me I had a friend request accepted: NO SHOE NICK HAD ACCEPTED MY FRIEND REQUEST! WHAAATTT? Why now? Why finally decide to accept it? This was a DISASTER. I had planned to spend my Saturday doing fun productive things. Him accepting meant I was going to spend my day sifting through his account with a fine-tooth comb. Looking for god knows what! But there he was. Photos of him. Such a handsome man. Such good teeth (yes, all this comes flooding back). He seemed like he used to be 'normal'. Looked happy in photos. Out drinking and being silly with friends. Hmm. What did this mean? Probably nothing. He had probably not been on there for months and wasn't thinking as far into this as I was. I needed to step away from Facebook. And his face.

That evening, Chris sent a message to say how he was looking forward to meeting me and he hoped he wasn't going to show off. But he warned me that he has that tendency. He seemed ever so sweet. I said I was looking forward to a catch up with my old mate Chris from school who I'd not seen in years. This seemed to put him at ease. Guess he was glad to hear I was still going on the 'it's not a date' theory.

So I got up the following morning and went to have a shower… and the next thing I knew, I was lying half on my bathroom floor, and half out of the bathroom on the hall floor. I had passed out. Full on fainted. This is not too unusual for me, I'm quite the fainter, but oh dear. It was pretty bad. I had to lie there for a long time while I came round. Waiting for the sound to come back to my ears, for my vision to become normal. To stop sweating and shaking. Seriously. What was wrong with me? This was worse than having root canal an hour before a date and having stroke face! My face was SO pale. I didn't know what to do. Do I cancel? No. I only fainted. No biggie. I'd just get in the warm shower and all would be ok. But I should probably eat. To bring myself back to normal. But I was meeting him for breakfast. Ok. I'd have a small bowl of mini Shreddies with some sugar and a tea.

Disaster. So so stupid. I had a word with myself, did lots of deep breathing and got ready. I covered my face in bronzer to hide my paleness and off I went to the café he'd suggested for breakfast. I got there ten minutes early. There was NO ONE in there apart from me and the two bar staff. No music either. This was going to be super awks. He walked in…

'Chris! Morning!' shouted the two girls from behind the counter. Oh. So they knew him. Even more awks. He came over to me, gave me a kiss on the cheek and said hi. He introduced me to the two girls who didn't seem to think it weird. They must have thought we knew each other. Great.

We ordered eggs Benedict. (I really wasn't hungry and still felt nauseous from the epic fainting episode.) He asked if they could turn the music up. Then he suggested we move to a different part of the café further away from them. This was making it SO obvious. But people kept appearing who all knew him. They all had dogs with them (which was odd) but even the dogs knew him! Little Gary the Chihuahua knew him. All wanted to come and sit and chat. He seemed VERY on edge. It was his own fault for suggesting places he clearly visits often and knows everyone!

So he said we should eat up and move over the road to a different café for coffee and cake. More food? (Do you not know I've passed out this morning and feel sick? Oh. You don't. Ok, yes, coffee and cake sounds great.) He did seem lovely. And the fact so many people clearly liked him was a great sign.

It turned out he knew the lady who bakes the cake across the road so they talked at length about some kind of Portuguese tarte… and he then ordered three (THREE!) cakes. Agh! Ok. We were able to chat more freely. He definitely was nervous and over-talking but I didn't mind this as it meant I didn't really have to think. It did genuinely feel like I was meeting up with an old mate. No awkwardness, no silences. All was good. We ordered more coffee. And chatted more about who knows what. Then he announced he needed to leave which was cool as it had been three hours (which flew by!) and he hadn't tried to lick my face – this was a bonus. He walked me to my car and said how lovely it was to meet me. I said 'likewise' and off he went. I wasn't sure he was someone I'd date. However, he was someone I'd be mates with. He was fun and funny. I would have liked to have some wine with him and have a good night out. But as for romance… Annoyingly, I didn't think it was on the cards. Which was lucky considering it was 'not what he wants'.

Chapter Twenty-Three

$$\text{---} \; \bullet \; \text{---}$$

In between all of this, it's vital you know that I had carried on seeing No Shoe Nick. It had kind of gone back to how it was. I saw him once a week. One week he even messaged to see if I was free on Tuesday AND Friday... What WAS this? I didn't push it. I continued with my awful online dating life because I didn't feel like I was doing anything wrong. Not yet. If I met someone who I'd like to date properly then OBVIOUSLY I'd stop seeing Nick. OBVIOUSLY.

Meanwhile, over on Tinder, there was Stuart who was performing in *Ghost the Musical* – touring with them and, at that time, in the show in Manchester. We matched. We had a friend in common – Simone (Rules Girl). I texted her to ask how she knew Stuart and what could she tell me about him. She told me he was lovely, a true gent and I should meet him. So we made plans to meet. (I was getting braver at this meeting thing!) He was pretty busy with the show so we planned to meet on a Saturday just before Christmas in between his matinee and evening performance. Ridiculously, my dad and step-mum were in the audience on the very same day. I OBVIOUSLY told them I had a date with him and to watch out for him (I screenshot his photo). I got texts CONSTANTLY throughout off my dad saying 'B says he's a dish. B says he's a good mover. B says he looks lovely'. Now, unfortunately, it rains most of the time in Manchester but this was a particularly bad rainy day. Like, REALLY bad. I was on the opposite side of town to where he was. I texted to ask where was best for him to meet. He replied commenting on the awful, awful rain. I kinda was hoping he'd suggest we re-schedule... I was going to turn up soaked. For just one hour of his time. My wish came true! He asked if we could move it as it'd be a nightmare for him. He seemed genuine and lovely and kept texting me all day/night telling me he wasn't bailing but was really looking forward to meeting me, etc. We planned to meet on the following Tuesday evening.

The Tuesday afternoon came. I was looking forward to it! I obviously had all the crazy things in my mind, like, 'Well, it's totally pointless as I'd never see him as he travels so much with the show. And it's a really anti-social job hours wise. But he could be the one. We could make it work... surely?!'

I got a text.

Stuart: Hey Shelly, I'm not going to be able to meet up I'm afraid. I met someone on Sunday and I'm going to see where it goes. I'm not really comfortable dating more than one person. Sorry for the late notice, Stuart. x

SERIOUSLY? The day after I was meant to meet you? You met someone? Like, TWO DAYS AGO? And you're basically closing yourself off?! WOW.

That's what I wanted to reply. However, I was pleasant and said:

Me: Hey, that's totally fair enough. I'd be the same. Good Luck! Hope it works out xxx

Now I think it was a lie. Because he changed his mind. But my mother tells me not to be such a Negative Nelly... so I have to believe it's real and that it's actually a nice thing that he's done that. WHATEVER.

Ok. Next.

I matched with Steve. Steve worked at the BBC near where I worked. He actually did a similar job to me. Brilliant. Instantly something in common. We chatted for a few days. Then he asked if I'd like to have dinner on Thursday. Why not? It's almost Christmas! May as well! So on the Thursday morning he messaged me asking where I fancied going and gave me his phone number. I obviously instantly check if he's on Whatsapp. It wasn't showing (what weirdo wasn't on Whatsapp in 2015?!) so I reverted to good old text messaging. I sent him a text... and got a notification to say it hadn't worked. I tried again, thinking it was my network. Nope. Message not delivered. So I returned to Tinder and messaged him saying it kept failing, gave him my number and told him to try me. He didn't reply. He also didn't text me. I never heard from him ever again.

Three months later he matched with my friend Sam... and pretty much did the same to her! AGAIN, WHAT IS WRONG WITH MEN?

*****

No Shoe Nick asked if I fancied a festive drink. For someone who doesn't drink, this felt like a breakthrough! Plus, at least one man wanted to actually meet up with me! So I met him in my local. We shared a bottle of wine. He freaked out. I could tell instantly. He was uncomfortable. It was odd. Maybe it was too couply and too normal for him. From that point, he went quiet. I didn't really hear from him. But I kept telling myself it was ok. He didn't owe me anything. He wasn't my boyfriend (sadly!), he didn't have to message me.

Christmas came and went… another one on my own with no lovely boyfriend. So I spent it with my lovely little nephews and sister to take my mind off it all. And I bought myself lots of nice presents to the value of £200 because that's roughly what I was saving by not having a boyfriend, right?!

It is, however, No Shoe Nick's birthday on Christmas day. So I texted him. Why not, I thought. He replied. Apologising for not getting in touch for a few days. We chatted a little bit then I carried on with the festive period, eating my body weight in cheese and drinking enough red wine to bathe an entire army.

New Years Eve was then upon me. UGH. Another one of those as a singleton, too. And I'd be entering a year where I was due to turn 35 years old. The year my other sister (the one who is the same age as me) was due to have a baby. As was my best friend Lucy which was the best, happiest news that I'd had in a long time. Yet here I was, on New Years Eve with nothing to do, no boyfriend. Again. I messaged one of my new best work buddies who had recently come out of an 11-year relationship. I asked what her plans are. She had none. 'GREAT! Come to mine. We can 'celebrate' together!' Literally ten minutes after we confirmed this plan, No Shoe Nick texted asking what I was doing as, if I had no plans, he'd come and see me. Telling me his options were either to stay in with his parents and probably going to bed before midnight or to go to a dinner party surrounded by couples and kids. Which he didn't want to do. (I get it. I also had similar offers which is very lovely but not really where a single person wants to be at midnight…) I told him he's too late as I had just made plans. Turns out my plans were actually fun! My lovely friend Arianne came over. We bought enough buffet food to feed about 27 people. We drank enough wine for that many people. We danced, we sang Auld Lang Syne, crossing arms and jumping up and down like lunatics. It felt like the best way to enter 2016. A whole new year. The year where I knew people would tell me '2016 WILL be your year' – I remembered them saying '2014 WILL be your year' and '2015 WILL be your year...'

Chapter Twenty-Four

So. How do I tackle this new year? The same way I'd tackled the previous? Do I continue online dating? What do I do about No Shoe Nick?

I originally went back to the plan about a year ago… and joined every website/dating app that there is.

I began with Happn. The idea is that if you cross the path of any single man who is registered on it, you get a notification of where you have crossed them. And how many times. It's a little stalker-y really. I try not to think too much about it. It makes you realize how many single men you walk past every day. Sadly, most of them I didn't notice and most on the app weren't really my type. Hilariously, there is a tram line running outside my office; I realized I was crossing paths with a man about 23 times a day… because he's a tram driver! Brilliant. Any handsome man I walked past and didn't realize, I would send them a message (if they'd ticked to say they also liked the look of me) but generally on this app, no one replied. It's weird, pointless and a huge waste of phone storage and battery. However, it's an absolute genius concept, and I obviously couldn't delete it because 'you never know' and one of my mates in work was about to move in with her boyfriend who she met on it so it MUST work.

I got a text from No Shoe Nick, wondering if I was free. He'd like to see me. I obviously would love to see him. So he came over. Everything felt different. Like he'd missed me or something. He'd hug me longer. Look at me in a different way. Something was definitely different. It felt really good. Really nice. He stayed over. Hugged me all night (even though I was way too hot and can't really sleep with anyone near me, never mind touching me!). It felt lovely so I went with it – as I do. He got up in the morning and went off to work. How lovely! Maybe all was actually going to be ok? And he had realised he couldn't live without me after all?! The next few days he messaged lots more than normal. I saw him more than normal. He stayed over on work nights. I tried not to get carried away. . .

One morning I got to work and, because it had just become something I seemed to do, I opened Happn to see who I'd passed on my way to work. THERE HE WAS. THOSE PROFILE PHOTOS I KNOW ALL TOO WELL. No Shoe Nick. On Happn. No no no no no no not again. HOW can he do this? Ok, I'm on there, but I'd made it pretty clear to him that I was going to continue looking – but he'd told me he didn't want a relationship with anyone! So what was he there looking for? He clearly (or so it felt) liked spending time with me. Liked me a lot. I'm not THAT stupid. I know what it feels like when a guy is into you or not. I felt like a broken record but I knew it'd eat me inside if I didn't know. So I texted him to ask.

Me: Hey. Sooooooo here I am with another honesty text... I didn't really want to message you again about this as I wanted to leave you to sort out your 'complicated' life before I asked you again. However I've just seen you on the awful Happn app which is obviously fine but selfishly I don't want you to go on dates with anyone else! Just me! So I thought I should re-tell you this. Not sure where your head is at with you & me – I should have just asked you last night when your response wasn't allowed to be 'it's complicated...'! When are you next free for a chat? x

I had basically forced a conversation on him about his life and told him he wasn't allowed to reply 'it's complicated' to things like 'where do you live?'

Nick: Hey. Understand. I'm away this weekend so will be free next week. Like we discussed in our previous honesty chat, I enjoy being with you but can't offer you the things I think you want.

He came round on the Tuesday. It was odd. Neither of us said anything. It was like we both didn't want to because we knew the outcome which really would mean not seeing each other again. Because once I'd heard this a second time round, I really would be stupid to keep hoping he would change his mind. We had a lovely night. Lying on my sofa. Hugging at chatting. But it was constantly in the back of my mind that we really needed to chat... we got into bed. He held me so tight and said, 'so I guess tonight wasn't the right night for us to have the honesty chat. Will you meet me tomorrow? But in a bar? And I promise we will talk.' I agreed and hoped I'd fall asleep. But I didn't. I knew this was probably the last time having him holding me in bed.

We met the following night. He looked sad. It went as I expected. He was so lovely – as expected. I told him I want to punch him and smash his head against a wall.

He said he'd felt guilty since Christmas. He had tried to want a relationship. If he wanted one, it'd be with me. But he just couldn't get his head around it. He said he'd got lots of emotions locked up inside and he didn't know why. He said he thought he needed some kind of major traumatic event to happen to make him let go and be 'normal'. He felt selfish that he was 'keeping me' to himself (although he said he knows that sounds arrogant) because he knows I deserve better. And that he was not good for me. He really, really wanted to be but knew he wasn't.

I told him maybe he just needs to let go and try it and stop fighting it – to stop being scared of the future. But he said he'd been fighting more trying to make it work.

I said it was obvious he enjoyed being with me and everything that comes with being with someone – with which he agreed. He really did love it. Massively. But he could only deal with it in small doses.

I asked what he was going to do in life – no cuddles, no sex, no one to do things with on weekends, no one to go on holiday with. Just himself. He said he'd lived without all that for so long he didn't need it. He said when he lived with his ex he used to sneak out for hours and go for walks on his own as he felt trapped and wanted to be alone.

The whole app thing was just the same as the Tinder thing – he showed me. He'd been on it for over a year. If you don't go on for months, they stop you from appearing in people's feeds but someone had 'charmed' him and he got a notification so he opened it and it re-activated it. I asked why he still even went on. It made no sense. He said to him it was like someone wasting time at an airport flicking through magazines with no intention of buying one. He just enjoyed looking at how ridiculous it all was.

I told him I was mad, angry and gutted. It's a huge shame to bond with someone and clearly connect with them but not do anything about it. It is just so frustrating to finally meet someone who you connect with, who likes you back, who enjoys your company a lot and you have lots in common with – but who can't give any kind of commitment! He wanted to want it. He wanted to want a life with me. Fucking annoying.

So that was that. I HAD to give him up NOW. I did this with Ed… and six years later I was still doing it! So this had to stop. Dammit.

Chapter Twenty-Five

Before that minor blip, I'd resolved to re-join every option. I even went back to Match and paid £30 for a month's subscription. January surely is a good time to be online dating? Everyone realises in January that they want change and want to be with someone... don't they?

I got matching and chatting to quite a few guys all at once. It gets ever so tricky!

One guy seemed perfect. Irish. Looked like Ronan Keating (who is my not-so-secret famous crush!) and he also had a few friends in common with me. One of them was one of my very good mates so I asked her a) what he was he like and b) how she had such a hot single friend and hadn't suggested we meet?

She also agreed I'd love him due to his similarities with Ronan. OMG! A recommendation and a good one! I carried on chatting to him. Funny. Lovely. Got loads in common. A few days later, my mate texted to ask how it was going with him (his name is Irish Phil). Great, I replied. She then said, 'you do know he lives in Belfast, right?' Somehow, SOMEHOW, I'd misread his initial message to me which stated he lives in

Belfast. For real? For actual real? WTF. Story of my bloody life. Either miles away or non-committal. (Or a psycho.)

Anyway, he went quiet. So that was that dealt with.

I braved it and opened OkCupid. This was the one I couldn't handle for more than 24 hours previously but my cousin met a guy on there (the first online date she went on and BOOM it worked. Damn her and her happy self!) so I decided to try again. Maybe it was different a year on?

Remember Stelios? The Handsome Greek? The one who wanted to be 'paypals'? Well, he was the first to send a message. It seemed he'd forgotten we'd spoken previously which kind of says everything about how many women he clearly meets. However, my mates convinced me it was a sign that he'd reappeared and maybe I should meet him so we swapped phone numbers. JEEEEZ he liked to text. And pester. I'd also forgotten how bad his English is (Ok, it was better than my Greek would be if I lived in Greece… but I don't live there) so after a few days of his persistent messages I decide again not to meet him.

The other 'delights' of OkCupid appeared. I'd forgotten this was an open app so ANYONE can message you…

CoxDT: Hi there, hope you doing well. You looks great im really interested. Would you like to be a friend.

BoooooHA: Can I ask you a few cheeky questions? Spit or swallow?

Ricardo90: Would you allow me to like your pussy on a first date.

KevYa: Happy Friday! Send nudes.

SimonDale34: Would you consider a 3some? I'm local. x

Hmm, yeah, so maybe it's no better?

Until I saw an actual attractive normal looking guy... I decided to send him a message. He replied straightaway and we got chatting. He did seem normal! By the end of a full day chatting, he asked if I wanted to go for lunch one day. This was perfect! It meant no pressure as I would have to leave lunch to return to work. So two days later, off I went to meet him for lunch. This felt new. A lunch date! In the middle of a working day! It also felt weird: I had all the weird panic, sick feelings I get before a date, and I was having them at work! The girls at work obviously thought this was brilliant.

There he was. Sitting outside the pub waiting for me. Taller than I expected. We instantly got chatting which was good. We ordered food (I'm really aware of time) and continued to chat. He seemed genuinely like a nice guy. He asked quite a lot of questions about my online dating life but I told him I only had an hour and I couldn't possibly cover it in it that time so I asked about him. And his past. He was 31. His name? Delightful David. He'd never had a girlfriend. I asked why. He has a very good job in the medical world so he spent most of his life studying. He went to university, got his head down, kept himself to himself and got a good job. He wanted to do well and keep progressing so it was just something he'd never had time to do or wanted to do before now. He'd been online for about two years and had seven dates. Two of the girls he met, he really liked but as he didn't know 'how to behave in relationships' he scared them off by being too intense. He was very open and honest which was nice. Refreshing! My hour was up so I had to leave. He asked if I'd like to see him again (I thought this was ever so brave to ask face to face) so I said yes.

We planned to meet the following Sunday.

What I hadn't realised was that this was Valentines day... Oh dear. Is this weird? Too much? Too odd? I sent him a text asking and he just said, 'It's just another day, don't think about it too much'. So wise! He was so right. A second date! This hasn't happened for a long time! Who knew it was ever possible again?!

*****

In the meantime, I carried on swiping over on Tinder and got talking to another two 'normal' guys over there. Was this THE week for online dating?

Firstly, there was Just Joel who seemed sweet. We swapped numbers (I'd become a lot more loose on giving out my number) and we chatted lots. He asked if I wanted to meet too... on the Thursday before my Sunday second date with Delightful David. It felt a bit wrong – but why not?

But there was also Nick. No, not No Shoe Nick. Normal Nick. Seemed ever so normal also. Normal is good. All I'm after is normal. Now Normal Nick was really funny and cheeky. I liked his chat. We swap numbers... and he asked if I wanted to meet... Oh lord.

And when? Sunday. Valentines Day...

Surely I COULDN'T do a date on the Thursday with 'JJ', then two dates on the Sunday? That's literally ruining romance... or something.

I asked everyone, including my mother who told me to go for it.

Just Joel and I made a plan of where we would meet. We decided I would drive over to near where he works as the traffic would be easier for me. I researched and found a pub that was only ten minutes for him to get to. On the Wednesday, the day before we were due to meet, he texted at 5pm:

Joel: Still on for 6pm?
Me: Yes, but tomorrow, right?

That would be a no.

He thought we had said Wednesday. I panicked. I'd been to the gym at lunch and hadn't rewashed my hair as I was planning on going to hot yoga that evening. I couldn't possibly go and meet him if I had got it wrong. I frantically scan backwards through messages... PHEW, I was right. He got a little mad as he had been sitting in the pub we'd agreed to go to for 30 minutes already. I told him he had the wrong day and I couldn't go that night. He said it was ok and it was his fault.

I decided to check the traffic as I'd have been leaving at the same time the following day to go and meet him. It would take me over an hour. I looked to see how the traffic would be for him if he came to me. Twenty minutes. So I messaged him to tell him this information. He replied to tell me he just wants an easy life and hates traffic of any kind so he'd really rather I drove to him... At this point I had a massive word with myself (as I do often) and realised that if he couldn't make the effort for date one, imagine how the rest of my life would be if we were to be married (hahaha yeah right) so I suggested we cancel and make plans for a weekend instead. Two months on, I was still waiting for those weekend plans...

At least that was one off my three-date list!

Normal Nick seemed funny. We had good funny random chats. We made plans for him to come to Manchester on the train as he's from Liverpool – now, THIS was someone who was making the effort to meet up with me on the first date!

THIS was how it was meant to be.

I worked out that I could meet Delightful David at 1pm, tell him I have dinner with my parents at 6pm giving me time to leave him and get to the date with Nick. All of this lying filled me with dread. With nerves! Imagine if Delightful David by pure random chance had a night out planned with some friends at the same place I'd be with Normal Nick. It's ok, I told myself: I'm not doing anything wrong. People do this. THIS is internet dating. THIS is how I should have been doing it all along. Cramming in as many as possible!

I arranged to meet Delightful David in a National Trust park. It was forecast to be nice weather. I was ignoring the fact still that it was Valentines Day. Just another day he said. I went to yoga in the morning to at least feel like I was doing something good that day. Something wholesome and nourishing...

We met at 1pm in the Visitor Centre. There he was, still tall. We did the awkward but polite kiss on the cheek and started to go for a wander. He is attractive, I decided – although I think I'd already decided this on date one. We walked for a very long time, chatting nonsense. Well, me chatting nonsense. I realised I was talking A LOT and he was politely replying so I decided to shut up and let him come up with some chat. Except it didn't really happen. Apart from with what felt like pre-planned questions such as 'what is the best holiday you've ever been on?' I got no feeling of anything... He was lovely and I was having a lovely time but something was missing. Was it just that he was still nervous? I don't know. We decided to go for tea and cake as it was cold and we'd actually covered about five miles. Again, we chatted for another hour or so but I realised he hadn't made me laugh at any point. I like to laugh. I like people who can make me laugh. Hmm. But he ticked all the boxes: he can cook (apparently), has a very good job, owns a house, is good looking, kind, polite... but DAMN IT.

What was missing? Maybe it WAS me after all? Here was a perfect guy who wanted everything I want but I didn't want him? Whhhhyyy? Maybe I could force it? Maybe he was a grower? We walked back to our cars (I'd obviously got my eye on the time because I was about to cheat on him and go on another date with someone else) and he said how much he enjoyed the afternoon and we should make more plans. I agreed with him. We should. By date three, I'll know... I told him to text me. Which he did. To say:

David: I had a really lovely day with you Shelly. Happy Valentines Day ☺

BLESS HIM! See! This was the kind of text I wanted off a boy! But I was just overwhelmed with the feeling of guilt.

At 5pm I realised I'd not heard from Normal Nick at all. I had texted him at 12pm to ask if we were still on for later. I waited, reminding myself that I was not to be walked on any more. If they really wanted to see me, they'd message. Hmm... should I get ready? Or should I wait? Yes, wait. 5.50pm came and I gave in.

Me: You're going to cancel on me aren't you? I can tell.

6.07pm:

Normal Nick: Oh I am, but with regret. I've felt awful all day (and have a strange rash) but that's no excuse for me being an inconsiderate **** obviously. That's a mindfulness 'fill in the swearword' exercise.

I replied with 'Knob? Twat? Dick? I luckily for you don't use the 'C' bomb...'

I then thought ok, I'd give him the benefit of the doubt as he was claiming to be ill so I said no worries and I hope he felt better soon.

Normal Nick: Do you want to do one evening this week? He asks cheekily.

I told him to let me know when the 'rash' had gone and we would make new plans. Much like Just Joel, I'm still waiting for those new plans.

So it turned out that after my panic of three dates in three days, it was over! PHEWF! Luckily men are rubbish (apart from Delightful David) and cancel on me meaning I couldn't whore myself out!

Delightful David continued to message me daily. However, it was all pleasant chitchat, about the weather, etc. If he were to ask me to meet up with him again, I would have, but he didn't. I think he was scared and waiting for me to ask but as I felt like something was missing I decided not to push it. I didn't want to give the boy the wrong impression. After two weeks of polite chat, Delightful David went away. This may have been an error? I don't know. But my gut told me he wasn't the one for me. I do genuinely hope he finds a nice girl as he was one of the nicest guys I'd met so far in this long and awful online dating road!

Chapter Twenty-Six

❧ ♥ ❧

Then there was Mike. Mike and I had matched on Tinder a few months back and chatted on and off. Then he started the chat back up. I remembered he seemed nice. We discussed meeting and he said:

Mike: Think it would be best for you if I met you somewhere close to you xx

YES! Again, another guy who isn't afraid to make the effort! He lived about twenty miles from me so I was pleased with this idea.

Me: I've got a family christening this weekend so my nephews will be here which is ace... However if you're free on Sunday about 6 (surely the christening will be over?) we could meet for a drink? x

This time, it was not a lie: I genuinely was busy in the afternoon and not on another date!

Mike: Yea I can do after 6 on Sunday no problem! xx

We were messaging up to the Sunday. On Saturday we hadn't made an actual plan of where we were going to meet but again I figured I'd wait for him to come up with a plan. It got to Sunday. It got to 19:37 on Sunday. I messaged:

Me: Sooooo it's after 6pm on Sunday...

This was becoming all too familiar. And then nothing. Nothing FOR ALMOST TWO WEEKS when I get a text off him…

Mike: Sooo it's 2 weeks since I said hi last :-/
Me: I think you'll find it's pretty much three weeks... Wasn't our date the best? We had such fun!

He asked how I was. Hadn't really got an excuse. Didn't bother to try to lie. Just said he was not sure what happened. I didn't reply. I was out – genuinely!
I got another text.

Mike: Hello? Yes?

Wow.

Me: You don't reply for almost three weeks then I don't reply for 20 mins & you're impatient.
Mike: I'm sorry I neglected you! Still would like to meet you though xx

I kind of forgot what had happened and reasoned I should

keep every door open because you never know. Don't burn bridges!

So the chat picked up again. After a week he asked if I'd meet him. Did I fancy a 'Netflix and Chill' night? I didn't really understand what that meant. People talked of it often. Was it a rude thing? Or literally just sitting and chilling watching TV? Maybe I'd Google it…

He then said things like 'you're being quiet' when I didn't reply for an hour BECAUSE I WAS AT WORK. I thought it was just girls who freak out and send texts like that? Also, I wanted to say, YOU DON'T ACTUALLY KNOW ME, WE HAVE NEVER MET, I MAY ACTUALLY BE QUIET!

Me: I'm mad busy.
Mike: Boooo what doing? xx
Me: Work x
Mike: Ooh you're moody! What you doing tonight? xx

Then proceeds to send messages, like, 'Are you alive?' if I don't text him before I go to bed. This is not what I need. This is verging on the craziness of the first man I met who had 'issues'…

Then:

Mike: It seems like you have fallen out with me ☹

This is way too needy. So I decide to stop this.

Me: I'll be honest with you: I've been messed around a lot by guys, letting them walk all over me. And I suddenly realised I'd let you do the same. I want to find someone who doesn't take the piss & disappear for three weeks when a date is planned. It's not the greatest start to anything. I'm looking to settle down & I don't feel like that's what you want. So I'm not sure making plans to meet up is a good idea. Sorry xx

I then get a flurry of messages over the next few hours and days…

Mike: That's exactly what I want actually! x

Mike: Sorry I messed you around it wasn't on purpose x

Mike: I wouldn't mess you around – I'd really like to meet you xx

Mike: Listen I am free tomorrow after 5pm same Sunday, Tuesday. Wednesday & Thursday I am free after 7pm and I am free after 5pm next Friday so if you want to go out the offer is there! I'd love to meet you xx

Mike: You going to take me up on my offer of a date or am I still enemy number one lol xx

Mike: Still chasing you Shelly! You alright? xx

Mike: Think I made a massive mistake with some of my banter with you the other weekend! You probably actually think I am a total tit and I am really not at all. It's my bad for being in a state in charge of my phone when I don't get in a state ever. Going to delete your number out my Whatsapp now as I am beginning to look quite desperate. Good luck!!!

Phew. Ok. He's gone! Thank goodness!

Chapter Twenty-Seven

A girl in work – a fellow online dater – says to me, 'have you tried Bumble?' Have I tried what? I had no idea what she was talking about. There's ANOTHER new app! Called Bumble. Within minutes it was downloaded to my phone. It's ever so similar to Tinder: swipey swipey, matchy chatty. HOWEVER, if you match with a guy, the girl HAS to start the conversation! It means no more thinking, 'ooh, shall I send a message first? Or shall I wait for the guy to send it? Do I look too keen if I send it first?' On this app I had no choice. Brilliant.

The first 11 men were the most attractive men I'd ever seen. I questioned if the app was real. It couldn't be. Those 11 men could not all be real. It was clearly a scam to pull girls in. Until BOOM... No Shoe Nick popped up. I obviously know he is real. And one of the most attractive men I've ever seen. He clearly still loved to be on the apps but with zero commitment to any girl. IDIOT. I pointlessly swiped yes on him knowing he wouldn't have done the same. He didn't need to rematch me – he already had my number and knew where I live...

So I got matching and started sending the first message. Shock horror, they didn't reply – and with this app if they don't reply for 24 hours, they disappear. This app was as bad as all the others! However, all my fellow single mates in London have had loads of success with Bumble.

And then Pete popped up. Paris Pete.

He replied! We got into an instant conversation about... biscuits! One of my favourite topics of conversation! He then went on to say:

Paris Pete: Surprised you are single, you're a fine looking woman and have a fond appreciation of biscuits – the essentials.
Me: I blame the fact men are stupid... oorrrrr not. I'd say 'why are you single' back but I know it's the worse question ever!
Paris Pete: Yeah we are pretty fucking stupid. But you know why I'm single.
Me: I do? Because you prefer Bourbons to Custard Creams?
Paris Pete: No, because I'm a male and I'm fucking stupid.

I liked him. He was silly and funny. We chatted lots about random stuff and decided to swap numbers. BUT there was a slight problem – a barrier some would say: he lived in Paris. He's from Manchester and was here for a family funeral when we matched. (I'm presuming he wasn't swiping during the funeral or wake. That would be inappropriate.)

He told me he was due to come back in a few weeks and we should meet up. He was trying to find a job back home. This could work! So we continued to chat until the weekend came when he was due to come over. And he didn't come. Hmm, I was starting to think this would be a waste of my time... He seemed genuinely sorry and said he would come over soon. His family live in Manchester so surely he'd be over to visit… nope. Never. We made friends on Facebook where he 'liked' all my photos but that's was far as the Paris Pete relationship was going. Maybe one day we'd meet but he's obviously not the one right now.

DAMN again.

*****

Back over to POF. (It's like an ongoing circle of life. But of online dating apps!)

I got this message:

Hi, having read your profile, I'm saddened that you haven't found that someone special. You're gorgeous and obviously intelligent, warm and caring. What's wrong with us men??!! I'd be over the moon to get to know you better.

From 'KPR12' aged 56.

Yeah… no.

Over on Tinder I rematched with Kevan, a guy from New York who plays the double bass in a band who I'd matched with months ago.

Me: You're back!
Kevan: Haha did we match last year?
Me: Oh. YES!
Kevan: Haha that's funny. Well, did we message?
Me: Wow. See how memorable I am?!
Kevan: Oh man. How embarrassing for me.

Yup. NEXT. Over on Match:

FreddiFun: Hey! If you want to meet up with me for some younger dick then I'd be up for it!

Ermmmm. I'm good thanks.
Tinder:

Jojohue: Hey you are really hot haha. I am kind of looking for a bit of fun on here. Realise that is not for everyone but if you think you'd be interested then let me know.

Now this guy looked beautiful. Tempting, but NO! I replied to him, saying I appreciated his honesty but it wasn't what I was after.

Seriously what was going on? Online dating has ruined love!

Staying on Tinder, I matched with IanIanIan and his opening message was this...

IanIanIan: Can you join me in burger king? This is my number ***********. Whatsapp me
Me: Join you in Burger King????
IanIanIan: Yes! Why not? Speak on the Whatsapp to me! I'm in Piccadilly. See you in Whatsapp. You should be quickly. Cause I need to go to Liverpool tonight to take the flight to Riga. I'm from Porto, Portugal.

Wow. Obviously I didn't speak to him on 'the Whatsapp' or meet him in Burger King. Who does that?!

Chapter Twenty-Eight

Then there was Gav. Or Thomas. He went by both names but I remain none the wiser as to why. We met on Tinder and he actually seemed normal. (I'm aware I use the word 'normal' a lot for all the guys I meet. Maybe that's where I was going wrong and I needed to move away from the 'normal'?) Normal were increasingly few and far between.

I liked his chat. He was funny. We appeared to be on the same wavelength. However he lived in Stoke. Yes, it was only 'about' an hour away from me but as we've discovered, I'm not a fan of 'long distance'... but I decided I HAD to have a word with myself: if my dream man was an hour away, then actually that was ok. So we swapped numbers and chatted on Whatsapp. Standard. His Whatsapp profile photo was different to any he used on Tinder and he looked good on that too. (I couldn't find him on Facebook, or Twitter, or the general internet because I didn't know if his name was Gav or Thomas and I didn't know his surname. He did well to lock himself down in the privacy world. My stalking skills meant I could usually find anyone!)

We chatted for a few weeks. It was obviously tricky to meet

up for just an hour after work for a coffee. However, I then re-membered I was going to Cardiff for a wedding. And I would drive past Stoke! So I suggested killing two birds with one stone, so to speak, and I suggested we meet somewhere near the motorway. He told me there were some gardens which I Googled and discovered there was a monkey forest there – what a date! I got up early and off I went. I told him before I set off that I'd have about an hour and a half with him to avoid the awkward 'yeah I've got somewhere to be' moment if it wasn't not going well.

I arrived in the car park. The place was HUGE. I called him and he told me I'd find him sitting outside the coffee shop wearing a big orange coat. I chuckled. I could see him from the car park. I got a bit giddy. But as I got closer to him... I thought, 'no. No, no, no. This cannot be Gav (or Thomas) he doesn't look ANYTHING like his photos. Is this why he wore a big orange coat? So I'd know who he was? Because he knows he doesn't look like his photos? The last time this happened to me, the man licked my face. I DO NOT want this experience ever again.'

He smiled at me, obviously recognising me BECAUSE I'M NOT STUPID AND I USE ACTUAL UP TO DATE PHOTOS OF MYSELF.

I didn't know what to do so I made a joke about his big aw-ful orange coat. He gave me a hug. Oh god. Oh dear god. He smelled. He smelled real bad, like of a boy who hadn't washed for a while. And he had a big out-of-control beard that I'm sure had food in. My stomach turned. I had told him I have an hour and a half. How was I going to manage this? He suggested we went for a coffee... IN THE GARDEN CENTRE. I didn't want to go anywhere with him at all but at least the monkey forest sounded fun! So off we popped to the garden centre. Ok, being a 35-year-old, I actually do enjoy a garden centre on a Sunday from time to time but on a date? Really? Wow.

He was actually ok to talk to. We had stuff to chat about, but the smell... the dirty look of him. Gross. I had to think it was ok. It was only an hour (and a half) of my life. We both drank our drinks (he got most of his cappuccino froth stuck in his beard), he looked at the time and noticed we still had 45 minutes until I had to leave.

'Fancy a walk around the little shops?' he said.

I, for some reason couldn't think quickly enough. 'Ok, yes.' WHHHHYYYYY? Why did I not say, 'No, I should get on the road to Cardiff'?

So we wandered and continued polite chat. He told me he had dogs (that may have explained why he smelled SO bad although I wonder if a dog may smell better than him) and that they were a huge part of his life. I decided to go OTT in telling him I really don't like dogs. Not at all. Nope. Nothing about them. I hoped that he would decide it wouldn't work between us and call it a day.

But it seemed not to put him off as he then suggested we go for one more drink before I had to hit the road. AGAIN I SAID YES! Jeeeeeeez what was WRONG with me? Too nice. Yes. I'm too nice. I needed to learn to not be so nice and just say, 'Actually, I'm going to go'. I don't even know what we talked about whilst I sipped my sparkling water as I was worrying about the fact all this liquid and having to drive on to Cardiff meant I was going to have to stop various times to go for a wee!

Finally the time came (pretty much to the minute) that I could leave. He walked me to my car and gave me another hug and told me it had been really nice meeting me. I think I probably said 'you too'. I'm SUCH a liar. I must stop lying. I got in my car and drove out as fast as I could. Thank GOD that was over. Then I suddenly realised I could still smell him. Because he hugged me TWICE. His 'aroma' was on me. On my coat. On my clothes. Maybe ON MY SKIN? And I had at least two hours to Cardiff. I stopped at the next service station to take my coat off and wash my hands and my face. No joy. He was still with me the entire journey.

I then worried about what I'd reply to him when he texted to ask if we could meet again. I thought loads about what excuse I could give him. This was not the point to start being honest and say, 'actually you really should think about washing and trimming that beard, and your hair'. I'd just say he was lovely and I enjoyed my morning (in a garden centre) but that I didn't think we had enough in common and we live far away from each other. And he had dogs. Yes. That would do.

I got to Cardiff and had to shower immediately. I had to wash him off me. I put the clothes including my coat into a carrier bag. I didn't want them near me until I can put them in a washing machine.

I went to the wedding, and the first person I saw? Ed. My ex. The ex of five years. We've had a good relationship since breaking up and stayed friends to a certain extent. However, the moment I saw him, I felt different – like it was his fault I'd just spent an hour and a half of my life in a garden centre on the motorway with a smelly man. Like all the disasters I'd had were his fault. Because if he'd have just manned up all those years ago, we'd probably be married with kids by now and I'd be like all my friends who 'don't understand how Tinder works'. Oh, to not know how Tinder works. What a lovely life that must be. So from that moment, the relationship with him changed. I didn't talk to him at the wedding. I didn't make plans to see him for a brew and a catch up the next day. I mainly wanted to punch him in the face so decided to stay clear. And we've not really spoken since.

And did Gav/Thomas text me? No! Did he think the smell was me?! How dare he not ask me out again?! It was me who was meant to reject him! Why on earth did he decide he didn't want to see me again? I was hugely offended! Maybe there WAS something wrong with me after all. Even a really gross smelly man didn't want to date me. I then had to realise I was lucky I didn't have to send a cringy message to say no thanks. Maybe my OTT dog-hate chat was the reason he had decided I wasn't for him. Yes. It was most definitely that...

Chapter Twenty-Nine

I got chatting to a guy who went by the name of 'Fitzy'. He said it was an old nickname from school which had never left him. He was a very good looking guy who does yoga and… he's a politician. Yes. I had found a politician. Brilliant. Through chatting to him, I discovered I'd already 'met' him… in a yoga class! About six months prior to finding him online, I'd been sitting waiting for my yoga class to start when in walked a handsome guy who I actually thought was No Shoe Nick. I did a double take. In fact, I think I did a triple take which instantly made me seem like a weirdo and, sadly for him, the only spare mat was the one next to me, the staring weirdo.

He was amazing at yoga, obviously. I spent the entire class trying not to stare at his muscles. It came to the end – the 'Savasana' which essentially is lying down in the dark with your eyes shut and relaxing for 5–10 minutes. The teacher comes round and gently massages your head and pushes your shoulders down. Unfortunately for me – and for the hand-some ever-so-good-at-yoga-not-No-Shoe-Nick boy – when she pushed on my shoulders, she moved my arms to a point where I was TOUCHING HIM! Now, during Savasana, you're meant to clear your mind and think of nothing. But all I could think was, 'oh my god. I'm touching the handsome boy who already thinks I'm weird. Do I move my arm? Or is that more awkward? Do I leave it there? I've now left it there too long to move it. Oh god.'. I decided after an awkward amount of time, to move my arm. When the lights came on at the end, he didn't seem fazed. He just smiled and off we went.

So I obviously decided that matching with him online was a SIGN (as I always do). I also decided not to tell him that I was the weirdo in that class.

It was in the weeks leading up to Brexit that he and I were chatting. I discovered that he was supporting the 'Leave' campaign. I was so undecided with which way I wanted to vote. Both sides seemed to have such good valid reasons as to whether to stay in the EU or leave. So I thought I'd ask him for good strong reasons why I should 'Vote Leave'. He was so quick with his response. He gave me his top five reasons. And they were great. I asked questions about some and his responses made me seriously consider voting leave.

We didn't discuss it again, but we'd become Facebook friends so I could see all of his involvement. I could also see him taking his gran out for lunch, photos of his and his family drinking champagne, photos of him at work... he clearly was a nice guy .

The morning of the Brexit result, I woke up early and looked at the news on my phone. We as a nation had voted out of the EU. What did this even really mean? It seemed no one really knew. The pound had dropped. Things looked and sounded bad. Terrible in fact. Then David Cameron quit. This to me didn't look like it was the right thing to do, to leave the EU. I decided to look at Fitzy's Facebook to see his reaction to the results.

We were no longer friends. The previous day we were friends and I saw him standing on the main shopping street in Manchester holding a 'Vote Leave' sign. But now it was all over… he'd deleted me. Surely not? Surely I was just tired and confused?

I spent the day in a panic like most other Brits. There were arguments in the office between the Vote Leavers and the Vote Remainers. It was a weird day – but I mainly spent the day in disbelief that he had deleted me! On the day of the results. I felt like he'd used his charm and his good looks – and internet dating – to pull girls in, sell them a great tale of why they should vote leave… then delete them! I went to the pub that night and had a few wines. I then got home and decided to send him a message:

Me: Evening. I have a question. It may be purely a coincidence that yesterday we were 'friends' on Facebook. I know because as you know I was undecided on what to vote so I kept looking at your profile & keeping up with your views as you seemed so passionate & to make sense. This morning after the news I thought 'I wonder how you celebrated' so I went to look. And you'd deleted me. I know we've never met & you just so happened to delete me the day of the results & this could all just be a coincidence but it feels a lot to me like you've been using online dating to pull girls in, to persuade/manipulate them as part of your campaign... And it doesn't feel right. Anyway, in the off chance I bump into you at a yoga in town, or in the pub. I'd hope it wouldn't be weird. And good luck with the rest of your journey in politics. You're clearly very good and very clever.

Go me! I was so pleased with myself. How dare he do this to girls? I bet most wouldn't have realized. HA! I'd caught him out!

However. He replied instantly:

Fitzy: Hi Shelly. Thank you for your kind words. I was awake most of the night so decided to have a clean up of my Facebook contacts. I have another Facebook account where my profile name is my actual name, Chris Tuner. This will be my public profile, my Fitzy profile is my personal profile. And yes, because we've never met, I decided to defriend you as we've not really been in touch. I'd be happy to add you on my public profile though of course! Hope you are well. The UK has a great future ahead.

Hmm, I'm not buying it. I, however, replied again, we chatted for a while; I told him that I actually voted to stay in so even if that was his plan, it didn't work on me. And that was the end of that.

Until a few months later... I was in a pub (again) and I saw him.

I didn't know what to do. I wasn't going to drink any alcohol that night but my mind was suddenly changed. I couldn't stop staring at him. There he was! In the flesh! My friends soon worked out I was distracted so asked me who the hot guy was that I kept staring at. I told them the story. They said I HAD to confront him. I don't do confrontation but I decided that it was something I really needed to do. After a few G&Ts I plucked up the courage. I went over to his table where he was sitting with two friends.

'Hi Chris' I said.

He looked at me, worryingly. 'I know you, don't I?'

'Yup.'

'Off Tinder, isn't it?'

Well actually, it was on Plenty of Fish but I wasn't there to remind him where we originally 'met'. He offered me a handshake. I took it, and gripped as hard as I could so he knew I meant business (I don't think he even noticed).

He said, 'You look even better in the flesh.'

'Wow, really smooth. You just look the same as your photos,' I replied. His mates sniggered.

He clearly recognised me but hadn't yet recalled our last conversation, clearly because he's chatting to a million girls all at the same time. We chatted pleasantries. About who we were out with, what our plans were for the night. I told him my plans were to go home after I'd finished my drink. He asked where home was.

'Wow, you really do have no idea who I am. Amazing.'

His friends sniggered again. He started to look a little mortified. Like the penny was dropping. 'I've got a new Facebook profile, why don't you find me on there, send me a message and maybe we can meet for a drink?'

'I'm ok, thanks. Anyway, I best get back to my friends,' (who I could feel were practically whooping back at the table where we were sat) 'but as I said in my message to you on Facebook, if I ever saw you in the pub, I wouldn't want it to be awkward so I just thought I'd come and say hi. Enjoy the rest of your evening.'

And I walked away almost laughing out loud at the whole situation. I felt like this was one online dating situation I had definitely won.

GO ME!

Chapter Thirty

Meanwhile, the dating messages were getting funnier but weirder.

BobbyJ43: You're 34, single, have no kids and you look like that... you're a unicorn

JammyJon: Hi you're very nice on the eye. Your name should be Google because you're everything I'm searching for. x

FutballFan3: WARNING!! PLEASE READ... if someone comes to your front door and asks you to remove your clothes and dance with your arms in the air... DO NOT do this... It is a scam. They just want to see you naked... Please copy and paste this to your status. I wish I had received this yesterday. I feel so stupid now...

Steveorob: Shells bells! How you doing? Trying a little downward dog or standing stalk (made that one up!) xx

Now, this I'd have replied to as we had matched on Tinder and he looked 'normal'. However, before he gave me time to respond, he sent another message:

Steveorob: I've got a willy warmer haha.

I went away for a weekend to my sister's in Lincolnshire to spend time with my nephews where life is simple and they don't know the word Tinder.

I decided to go for a run so went to open the Map my Run app. It's blue in appearance. Unfortunately it looks like the POF app and I clicked on it so it activated my profile in that area! DOH! Oh, well, I reasoned. I'd just close it. No harm done. It would be pointless matching people in that area, it being four hours away. If it didn't work with Paris Pete, it wasn't not going to work with someone in Lincolnshire!

Then I got a message:

Matthew: Hey... what are you doing this way?

WTF. What the actual? How? Matthew is Matt. Matt the Crazy Firefighter. The mentalist I met first. How has he found me? Where IS he? He was meant to be in London?

I replied out of intrigue.

Me: Hi. I'm visiting my sister and the boys.
Matt: I tried to add you on FB but I guess you don't want that. I can't believe you're still single. Hope you're well, still think of you all the bloody time. Am loving life in London, doing a Personal Training course now and moving back to Manchester next year. Can't wait, running bootcamps with my old group and working in a gym too.

Me: How come you're moving back if you love it? Why aren't you carrying on in the fire service?
Matt: I miss my friends there and I'm always back up that way. I've tried to meet up with you a few times when I've been back but you've always dodged me. I messaged you loads on Facebook but you never reply. We don't have to speak anymore if you'd rather? I'm a big lad, I can take it.

Well, for starters, he'd NEVER messaged me on Facebook. I am not stupid. I even know about the secret inboxes. Also, we never spoke anymore anyway so I wasn't sure what that even meant. I sat and breathed for a while. And then did something I should have done years ago:

Me: I've no messages at all. Yes, I had a friend request from you but I chose to ignore it. Why would I want to be friends with someone on Facebook who can see my entire life, who two years ago ruined my self esteem, called me a slag on numerous occasions, constantly put me down, constantly accused me of dating other people, told me my friends are shit, made me feel unworthy of anyone and anything. You ruined my sister's wedding for me. You ruined my birthday. You ruined me, Matt. I was happy. But now I'm still broken. I try and I try to move on, to forget everything with you. But I struggle. And it's not nice at all. I think I'm doing ok then you pop up again. A constant reminder of that awful time in my life. So actually, yes. I'd rather you left me alone to let me find my peace. I know you've said you've had good counselling now and you're doing better, and I really hope you are. But I really hope

you don't do to anyone else what you did to me. I
hope wherever you end up, that you can find your
own peace and happiness x

I pressed send. And sat and cried. And cried and cried.
With a huge sense of relief. Never before had I been brave
enough to say it to him. It felt weird, it felt sad but, ultimately, it
felt good. Hopefully this time he really would get the message.

I blocked him on all forms of social media. I came off all
dating apps. I locked myself down. For a bit of protection. My
heart needed some protecting and this felt like the only way.

Chapter Thirty-One

A few weeks later, I was at work and my friend Amy said, 'So, I was out last night at a Take That gig, and my friend Ollie was there. He happened to ask if I had any nice single friends… and suddenly everything made sense. You and him are perfect for each other! I don't know why I've not thought about this before!'

She summoned me over to her laptop to have a look at photos of him. He was hot. Really hot. How had she never mentioned him to me before?

'Shall I give him your number?'

I pointed out that he may not want my number.

'Oh, he does. I showed him your photos on Facebook.'

Oh. OH!

Within about three minutes of giving him my number, I had a text:

Ollie: Hi Shelly, it's Oliver. Cupid Amy has passed on your number, ha! She was singing your praises on Tuesday night and said I should get in touch. You having a good day? You up to much this weekend? x

We instantly hit it off. It was like I was texting one of my best mates. It was fun, it was constant. It was good chat.

We made plans to meet on a Sunday afternoon. The plan was to drink gin. In the run up to meeting, we continued chatting. I couldn't believe Amy had never told me he existed before. AND he lived in Altrincham, the next town to me... just eight-minutes' drive away! WINNER! How had we never bumped into each other?

I don't usually like to overthink what I wear when I go on a date, but this one felt different. Different perhaps because he wasn't off the internet and in photos he looked like a guy who dresses well. So I went shopping and bought a new outfit. Nothing OTT. I didn't want it to look like I'd made too much effort. I was pleased with my purchases. Perfect for an afternoon in the sun drinking gin.

I realised the was the finals of the Euros on the same day and he's a football fan so I texted him:

Me: Realised the finals of the Euros is on tonight... Which I guess you'll want to watch? So shall I come over your way so it's easy for you to go watch? I'll just jump back on a tram & leave you to it?

He told me that was very thoughtful and suggested he'd come and pick me up. What a gent! This was new! He said that way it'd maximize our time.

So he turned up in my car park. I had that panic of 'what do I do when I get in his car? Usually I give first dates a kiss on the cheek' but decided whatever naturally happened would happen. And I needed to make sure I didn't fall down the stairs out of my flat as he was sitting right in front of the window and would be able to see everything. Oh god. PANIC! Calm, keep calm. So off I went, trying to casually and sexily walk down my stairs into the car park (can you even walk sexily downstairs? I'm pretty sure there was nothing sexual about my stomp down) and I got in the car.

He leant across to kiss me on the cheek and said, 'Nice to meet you'. Phew. Ok. Great. That was ok. We chatted all the way to the pub like we had known each other for ever. General normal chitchat. And that was how the date continued! It was brilliant. The weather was perfect. We sat outside the lovely markets in Altrincham on the benches, drinking gin cocktails. They were going down swimmingly. I can't even tell you how many we had as it was all just so brilliant and smooth and natural... until the bar staff came to tell us they closed at 6pm. We were then at that awkward point in a date where neither knows if the other one wants to carry on. I wanted to carry on and the vibes he was giving me said he wanted to carry on.

'Shall we go somewhere else?' I said. SIMPLE. And he said yes.

We went to another ace bar, ordered more gin and headed to the beer garden. I was suddenly aware it was now a bit chilly. I tried to hide it, but I'm quite the goose-pimply person so he suggested we move inside. I was so happy with this that I immediately got up and went inside without a second thought to my bag or my coat. I was showing signs that I was pretty wasted. Uh oh! Thankfully he found it hilarious, went and got it all for me and suggested I ate some crisps. The chat and the laughs continued to flow. I had zero idea what time it was, until a television in the bar was showing the football. I was meant to have left him by now so he could go and watch it with his friends. AGHHH!

Sheepishly, I said, 'Um, are you aware that the football has started? I should go so you can go and watch it!'

'Yes, I'm aware, don't worry. I'm having more fun here. I'll watch the highlights when I get in.'

I practically melted in my chair (I probably almost fell off it). No guy ever does that! After a few MORE gins and some crisps, he suggested we went to get some proper food. We went to a Thai restaurant. It's at times like this that I'm so thankful I've been to places like Thailand so that I don't look like a complete idiot when I have no idea what to order! Thankfully, I was actually able to teach him about a few dishes to the extent that we decided to get a few to share AND a bottle of red. Uh oh, I thought. I must remember it's Sunday night and I have work tomorrow. But I'm having such a lovely time! With a boy! Who is a friend of a friend therefore not a complete lying mentalist off the internet! And a handsome friend of a friend, too. I did not want it to end. The staff in the restaurant, however, did. We didn't notice that we were the only ones left and they were waiting for us to finish the wine so they could close. Oops.

It really was late by this point. And I'm sure I was probably chatting absolute nonsense but in the hope that he was, too, so he wouldn't notice. He walked me to a taxi, gave me a kiss on the cheek and thanked me for a lovely evening, telling me to text him when I got home.

I tried to play it cool and wait at least 11 minutes after I got in to text him.

Me: I'm home! Thanks for a lovely afternoon/evening... Sorry you missed most of the football but hope my gin chat was worth it. Let me know when I can return the favour of drinks & food xx

(He wouldn't let me pay for anything, which I don't like; I like to pay my way so I kept telling him this. He kept agreeing that NEXT time, he'd let me pay.)

Ollie: Hola! Thank you! I had a really nice time, great company and not arsed about the football. Gin chat was definitely worth it! When you thinking? I'll happily sack the gym off to go out ;) x

Agh! What was happening? This was all too good to be true! Then he texted again:

Ollie: You're also stunning!
Me: Stop it... (You're not too shabby yourself.)
Ollie: Oh behave! Take a compliment.
Me: You have a good pair of eyes, FYI.
Ollie: Thanks! I was thinking exactly the same about yours. I was going to mention it but didn't want to sound cheesy.

Wowzers. All this time I'd wasted with swiping left and right, but if only I'd been out wandering a few miles from my house, I may have bumped into him! Madness. HOWEVER, I remind myself that it had only been one date and I MUST. NOT. GET. EXCITED. I decided to stay neutral…

So we arranged to meet the next bloody day! After work, of course. He wanted to go for a run. I, however, knew I'd be way too hungover to run. Silly idea. I suggested we go for a walk if the weather was as nice. Even the thought of a walk was a bit intense with the size of the Monday hangover I had.

We spent all day texting and arranged to meet at his place straight from work. It took me longer than planned as I got stuck in a mass of traffic. And I started to really need a wee. Hmm. I was already late. If I stopped somewhere I'd be even later. And I was so close to his house. I decided the only thing to do was to use his bathroom on arrival. Although I wasn't sure if the plan was for me to even go into his house… I decided to text him:

Me: I'm stuck in traffic and I really need a wee. But I'm not far away. Please may I use your bathroom?

I was hoping that didn't come across as the weirdest chat up line ever and that he knew that I genuinely did just want to use his bathroom and not use it as a way to get into his house and molest him. Ha. As if I'm even capable of that.

When I got there, he was waiting with the door open and said, 'It's upstairs at the top. You'll see it'. I said thanks and ran past. Date two. Nailed it, right? Hmm. I only had a word with myself about this once I was in his amazing bathroom. With its free-standing roll-top bath. And lovely sink. And nice floorboards. And amazing photos on the walls. And very well decorated. Oh dear. I was probably not doing myself any favours. This guy clearly had very good taste, and just from seeing his bathroom I could tell he had a very lovely house! I MUST STAY NEUTRAL. I MUST NOT IMAGINE MYSELF LIVING HERE. NO NO NO.

I found him downstairs in his equally lovely kitchen. Honestly. This guy really was too good to be true.

We started walking and chatting. As with the previous day, the chat was still there even though a) I'm massively hungover (he doesn't appear to be) and b) there is no gin involved! We walked and walked and walked. He then realised we'd walked a long way. About three miles from his house, meaning we had to walk three miles back. I didn't mind at all – other than the fact I was starving. But it was ok: I was walking with a boy who seemed to be more than happy to walk with me.

We finally got back to his and he invited me in for a cup of tea and some biscuits. Ideally I'd have liked a full-blown meal but I went with it. I didn't want to cut it short and he clearly didn't either. And I LOVE biscuits so I'd happily take that as a meal.

We sat in his beautiful lounge watching TV and continuing to chat nonsense. It got to 10pm and I decided I really should go home but instantly get the fear of the goodbye, thinking when I say bye, I'd quite like a cheeky snog, but how do you do that? Hmm. Again, I must not panic and let whatever happens, happen. We got to his front door, he opened it, and gave me a kiss... on the lips. One that couldn't be classed as a peck – but also couldn't be classed as a full smooch. Whatever it was, it was lovely. And I wanted more. But NO. MUST. STAY. NEUTRAL.

Again, he asked me to text when I got in. I waited approximately nine minutes this time...

Me: I'm home!! And I didn't have to use a satnav! Wooop! Thanks for a other lovely evening xx
Ollie: Hey beautiful! Awwww, well done you! I've just jumped into bed. Feel like I'm going to have a good nights sleep, hee! I really enjoyed our evening too. Sorry if the walk was a bit of a mission! x

The chat continued, every day. He texted as much as I did which is always a bonus! No games. No nonsense. If you want to text, text. If you don't, don't. It was all so simple! How it should be! He'd text funny things, nice things, general normal life things. I could not believe my luck! So I decided to put the lottery on... and woke up to an email telling me there was news about my ticket! Woooo!!! I logged on... £2.80. Ok. Not what I was hoping for but better than nothing.

We discussed when date three would be. He had loads on with training for a half marathon, he worked in a bar on a Friday night and obviously had friends (or not so obviously if I look back at some of the mentals I've met online who are friendless). He said he'd happily sack off seeing some friends on the Thursday if it meant he could see me. Wow. He was saying all the things I'd dreamt of for so long! But I told him no. I'm a firm believer in not binning off friends. They're very important. So instead we agreed that we'd see each other on the Wednesday after he'd been to the gym. He came over to mine and we chilled on the sofa watching TV... until he went in for the smooch! FINALLY. And it was everything I'd been hoping for! It's always a huge let down when you fancy someone, then you go in for the snog and it doesn't work. This worked. And worked well. Another tick for him!

Everything continued in this same easy, brilliant way for weeks. It was great. He started staying over. I also continued putting the lottery on! The following week I won £10 and the weekend after... ONE HUNDRED AND THIRTY FIVE POUNDS! I really did feel like I was the luckiest girl in the world. I suddenly knew what people meant when they said, 'you never know what's around the corner, and when it happens, you'll know.' I felt like it had happened. I couldn't have been happier.

My mate Amy was so pleased with herself. She said, 'I don't actually see what can go wrong. You fancy each other. You're both nice. You're both normal. This is amazing.'

I'd been away for the weekend to Cardiff. We had made loose plans to go for a Sunday Roast Dinner Date when I got back. I texted him to say I was home and what was the plan.

This was the response I got:

Ollie: I want to be honest with you and I just don't think I've got the time at the moment to be seeing someone. I thought that's what I wanted but as you can see I've got a lot on and I just don't want to waste your time, sorry x

Wow. Just wow. How does someone go from clearly being into you and texting loads to that? Makes. No. Sense.

What do I do? What could I do? There was nothing I could do. SO random. And also rude. Who just drops someone on a text? Especially someone 'normal' who is a friend of a friend. I was gutted. Proper gutted. I thought I'd hit the jackpot (I almost did with my £135 lottery win!). It blew my mind. Yes he was busy. But not THAT busy. And surely if you like someone, you find time. Just a little bit here and there? We only lived eight minutes away from each other. Wow. Who knew? I wanted to reply. But I didn't know what to reply. My mother, bless her, came over to give me a hug and we drafted a text. About eight times. No, maybe more.

Me: I knew this was too good to be true... the last few weeks has been fun & silly. We get on really well & seemed to be on the same wavelength. Like you I also have a lot on & that's because I've had to keep myself busy for years as a singleton having come out of a long-term relationship that went horribly wrong. However, because I don't want to be single forever, I turned to evil internet dating & I've ended up just being messed around a lot by guys. When I met you I realised pretty quickly that you're not like any of them.

So I'm not gonna lie, I'm gutted. Especially as I know you're not a murderer off the internet & you happen to have a good face & lovely long eye lashes x

We sat and we waited for him to reply. Eventually, my mum could no longer stay awake so she went home to bed but told me to text her AS SOON as he replied. He never ever did.

Ho bloody hum.

Gah.

Hmm.

I REALLY don't want to go back to online dating. If nothing else, having this time off has been so nice! I've had time to do stuff and my hand hurts less!

Chapter Thirty-Two

It was now the beginning of September 2016 and I suddenly realised I had 12 days' holiday left. And as usual, no one to go away with. So I had a moment. That moment involved me Googling 'guided tours in Bali'. Ever since I watched *Eat Pray Love* many moons ago, I'd had the biggest need to go there. And right now, I felt like Julia Roberts in that movie. I then Google 'best time for weather to go to Bali'. I learned that October was the start of the rainy season so I had a week to go before it'd be too late.

I asked around. Did anyone want to go to Bali? It would be sunny. It would be great! Anyone? Or if not Bali, anywhere? I could go to Bali another time. Anyone? ANYONE? No? So, should I go alone? Should I do this? Just me. Little old me? To the other side of the world? On my own?

Yes I should. When pretty much all your friends are now married off with small children, it seems it's the only way.

Within two weeks of this crazy Googling moment. I was in Bali. VERY surreal.

Everyone said cliché things like, 'you'll go and find yourself', 'you'll learn so much about yourself', 'you'll meet so many amazing people like yourself', 'you may even meet the man of your dreams who is doing the same thing'.

I had no idea what would happen but was not expecting any of that. I spent 16 days pretty much on my own. My guided tour involved myself, a guide (Suki), a driver (name never known) and a couple from Denmark: Winnie and Jonnie who were 65. My mum would text everyday: 'are you part of a big group yet?' Nope. Just me and Winnie and Jonnie. In fact, some days I didn't even see them. The trip involved five hotels. We were picked up and taken to a new part of Bali every other day. And en route we'd stop off at places of interest. Like temples and monkey forests. So I'd see them in the car, bump into them at temples and then not see them for a few days as they were in different hotels to me.

Some days, the most I said out loud was 'cereal and tea please', 'chicken satay and a litre of water please', 'chicken nasi goreng and a bottle of Bintang please'.

But it was so great! Yes, there were lovely young couples everywhere on honeymoon happily in love, and there I was living my own *Eat Pray Love* moments, pretending I was Julia Roberts cycling through rice fields. I didn't need a man to go on holiday. This was the best holiday ever! I could get up whenever I wanted, go the beach if I wanted to, stay by the pool if I wanted, go wherever I wanted for lunch and dinner. Go to bed at 9pm if I wanted. (I mostly did that like a massive loser.)

I didn't 'find myself', I didn't 'find the man of my dreams', I didn't 'make loads of new friends' (other than Winnie and Jonnie) but I did have an amazing time. So there.

On the way home I debated a few things. Mainly, do I go back onto online dating? Of course. My one true love.

I decided that I've proved to myself that I can have a great time on my own so maybe I'd give it one serious final last chance. Then going into the New Year, I'd be done. I had been off it for quite some time now. My fingers and thumb had had quite the rest.

Chapter Thirty-Three

❧ —♥— ❧

The first guy I got chatting to – Gary – seemed quite normal but ever so familiar. I showed a picture to my friend Sam, my single mate who I went on the awful speed dating with. Her first reaction? 'Is there a photo of him with a puppy down his top?' Yes! Yes, there is! Of course she recognised him. Us online daters get recognising everyone nowadays from the world of online. She hadn't dated him; however, one of her friends had been chatting to him but he sent her a message to say he'd met someone and he didn't want to mess her around. Fair enough. It obviously hadn't worked out with whoever that was so he and I continued to chat. Then he went quiet – standard. THEN I got the following message:

> **Gary:** Hiya. Sorry for the crap response rate. Met someone over the weekend who I'm going to see how it goes. Not the type of bloke to multiple date. Sorry to muck you about.

So he was one of those: meet someone, fall in love within a day. Then four days later, I get a message:

Gary: Soooo hi. It didn't work out as planned. Would you still like to meet for a drink?

Not really, no.

The random messages then start coming back. Oh how I've missed them.

Manhot45: Hello my dear how are you? Your profile picture really take my attention to you so much, I hope we can share some nice words.

Risley: Hi would you be interested in a male to serve. Would do all chores and also give any worship. Nothing expected in return.

Er. I'm ok, thanks...

Jaykeybabey: Hi gorgeous wow you're so beautiful you're one of the most beautifulest girls on here you're just so unreal you're the actual definition of perfection wow.

If you could see this man, you'd run a mile.

Colinpr2: Hello Shelly. How are you? Your profile seems really nice so I thought I would send you a message. I do have one question though... how on earth are you single? You didn't do something terrible in a past life did you??

Again, run away. Far, far away.

JonnyT: Hi shelly, how are you and hope weird people aren't putting you off? x

I looked at his profile and two minutes later I get another message off him:

JonnyT: Ah you stopped by but didn't say hello ☺ well good luck on your search

Wow. People will forever amaze me.
Within minutes it happened again:

SexySte987: Hey how are you? Amazing smile.

Four minutes later:

SexySte987: Am I not your type?

Seven minutes later:

SexySte987: Was only being nice.

Then there was Liam. Suspicious Liam. We chatted. He seemed lovely. Been in a relationship for six years and for one reason or another they broke up. He'd been single a year. Has a good job in engineering. We chatted and chatted and seem to be on the same path. He suggested chatting off the app.

'Sure!' I said. 'Here's my number – Whatsapp me' – which is a standard online dating line.

He said he didn't use Whatsapp. Text is fine, I said. He then told me he had three phone numbers due to bad signal at home and at work. This is when I started to get suspicious). WTF? He said he didn't have reception at his home to use text messages. Fine. Then just be normal and use Whatsapp like LITERALLY everyone else in the country.

He sent me this:

Liam: I have friends and family message me on Telegram as that works across all my devices with a single account. Try it, it's like Whatsapp but better. (Whatsapp doesn't work on more than one phone with a single account.)

Me: I'm an honest person so I'll be honest with you... I'm not sure asking a girl to download an app to be able to chat outside of this app is going to work for you... we may as well just carry on chatting on here? I'm more than happy for you to message me on the number I've given you but I have all the apps I want and need at present. Hope I don't sound like a knob for saying it, but I just thought I'd be honest.

Liam: What works for you doesn't work for me because I have three phones which has practical restrictions. I don't understand what the problem is.

At that point I decided he was already too complicated so I moved on.

I then got this off someone:

SiTall5: There once was a girl named Shelly, she liked to watch the telly. She went on a date, which turned out to be great, now she's going off to Delhi.

Now this I LIKED! Shame he looked super weird! But I felt the need to congratulate him on his creative ways anyway.

*****

I was chatting to a guy called Darren for a few days on POF, he was from Sale too. Nice and easy! He was sporty, liked the great outdoors, seemed funny. It got to a point where I thought he's going to ask if I wanted to meet him – which is the point I question how much DO I want to meet him? Can I be bothered? That day I was in Sale, in the queue in Boots waiting to pay for a curling wand (I don't know why I was buying one, I have many items like this that I use once then realize I'm crap at doing hair and never touch it ever again) and there he was! Darren! From Sale! In the queue three people behind me. AGH! Had he seen me? He doesn't really look like his photos, I thought; I don't fancy him in any way shape or form. AGH! What do I do? I decided to stand VERY still facing forwards in the hope he hadn't noticed me. I had never stood so still in all my life. The lady was taking forever to work the till. Come on lady! This could be ever so awkward!

'Would you like a bag?' she asked.

'No! Yes! No! Erm! Whatever is quickest! No? NO! I'm good thanks!' I pay and dart. It was like the fastest date I've ever had but without having to speak to the guy. At least I saved myself a Saturday night rather than having to go on a date with him. I then became one of 'them' as I didn't send him anymore messages. And he didn't send me any to be fair. Maybe he saw me and had the same thoughts. If only all online potentials could appear in queues behind me in shops. It'd save a lot of time and money!

*****

Then I chatted to Scott. Scott Snake. No, not for any rude

reasons – I did not see his snake thank you very much – but because he said he liked all things beginning with 'S' including snakes and people called Shelly.

His humour was my kind of humour. Very random. Very silly. We chatted pretty much constantly for a week. We swapped numbers, etc. He lived in a slightly awkward place that didn't make meeting easy. So one Saturday night he texted me as he was in a village quite near to where I live asking if I fancied meeting up with him and his friends who were on a couples night and he was a gooseberry. I turned down the offer, mainly because I was in my PJs on my sofa under a blanket like every other Saturday night – and also it would be 100 per cent weird to go on a first date where the guy is out with mates. I said if he was around the following day maybe we could meet for a coffee before he headed home.

He suggested we meet in Manchester city centre so that he could go straight from the train after our date. I told him to pick a café and I'd meet him there. However, he picked a café in a new, very trendy part of Manchester where I ALWAYS get lost, even with my satnav on my phone so he suggested meeting me off the tram. He'd be waiting in Piccadilly Gardens. His photos, including his Whatsapp photo, were of a big, muscular, handsome man. As the tram pulled into the stop, I almost laughed out loud. I instantly spotted him. A weedy, nerdy boy sat waiting for me. Oh. Oh dear. How disappointing. I could have continued on the tram and not get off but that would be mean. And hey, it's not all about looks! He was very funny on text messages so I'd just go with it. Maybe I'd fancy his humour. Nope. Ok, he was nervous (I was SO over being nervous on dates by now. I would just treat them as if I were meeting new clients at work for the first time) but he didn't have that humour. He tried to crack jokes that are the kind of jokes my dad does. I've had 35 (and a half) years of those. I don't need any more thanks.

We finished our coffees and when he said 'shall we go somewhere else?' everything inside me was saying, 'just say no. Just say no, say you've got somewhere to be, say you've got shopping to do, you don't want to have to sit and listen to his jokes any longer. Just be honest and say no.' What comes out of my mouth? 'Yes, sure, why not?' WTF is wrong with me? Why can't I just say no?

We went to the bar next door. He had a lemonade and I had my standard date drink: a sparkling water. To be fair, some things we chatted about were quite interesting but was I leading him on? Why didn't I just say no? I'm such a wuss! Too bloody polite for my own good! Finally (after another hour and a half) he said he should probably make moves as he had a train to catch and we part ways.

Chapter Thirty-Four

On the tram on my way home, I made a very strong decision. It went like this: I've tried online dating for almost three full years and it hasn't worked for me. I think it's time to give up. It's clearly not the way I'm going to find my prince charming. Maybe I need to leave it to fate and the universe. It's more often than not a disappointment and a waste of four polite hours of my life. So on 30th October 2016 I decide enough is enough. I got home and opened my apps one by one. (Ok, ok, I am on five. That may be classed as desperate/looking too hard? But you've got to be in it to win it, right?!)

I usually just disable my profiles as it makes it easy when I want to go back on them. No need to fill all the details out again, choose eight photos again blah blah blah. But this time it was different. I fully closed them down. They all give you a warning: 'Are you sure?' Yes. I clicked yes on them all. I am sure. Delete account. Delete account. Delete account. Delete account.

I got the final app to close down. POF. I hadn't opened it for a few days as I'd been busy talking to Scott Snake. I noticed I had 16 messages in the inbox. I opened it and couldn't be bothered to read the messages as I could see the photos of who they were from. Mainly 54-year-old pervy men. As I was about to come out my inbox page, I saw a face mixed in there. A handsome face. A message from a handsome man. Uh oh. Do I open it? I'm on here to close this nonsense down! What do I do?? I don't want to get into this. To go through the chat. I'm DONE, damn you, I am done. But, what if? I mean, it may be a weird message. And his main photo may just be a particularly good photo. Ok, I may as WELL open it... it would be rude not to.

Martin: Hey, you have a beautiful smile. Why are you single??

Hmm. Lots of them say that. I looked at his profile. (WHAT AM I DOING? I'M SUPPOSED TO BE CLOSING THIS AWFUL THING DOWN!) Oh. He looked handsome in all photos. Ok. I looked to see what he'd written. If he'd written 'will fill in later' it meant he was just a player and out to chat to anyone.

His headline: Fancy Making Memories?

35 from Manchester
Intent: Looking for a relationship
Body type: Athletic
About me: Looking for a fun easy-going girl who's not too tall, with an infectious smile. Oh and not too keen on girls that hide behind heavily layered masks of makeup... subtle amount is more than enough.
I'd very much like to share my life with someone caring, considerate and loving who I can make many memories with. Am I describing you?

Erm. Yes. Yes you are.

I also noticed he had THE yellow dot next to his photo. This is PRECIOUS information in the world of POF. It meant he PAYS TO BE ON THERE! No one pays to be on there unless they really mean they're looking for love. (It's pointless paying. You get no added bonuses as far as I can tell, so maybe he was actually stupid?)

Uh oh. Maybe it was fate? I couldn't ignore it. Could I? Maybe this was how it was meant to end? Just as I was giving up... he appeared?

I HAVE to reply.

Me: Hi Martin. I'm single because I keep meeting absolute weirdos. How about yourself?
Martin: Snap.

We chatted for a few days. I obviously didn't tell him I only opened the app to close it down, and in the meantime I ignored all the other messages from all the other weirdos. He then suggested we go for a drink 'when he gets back'...

Me: Why, where are you?
Martin: Maldives.

Maldives? What 35-year-old single man goes to the Maldives? And who was he with? Hardly a location for single guys to go. I don't ask. It's nothing to do with me. He's on holiday. I don't know him. Whatever.

We swapped numbers.

I can't help myself.

Me: So... why the Maldives

Martin: My ex picked it.

Me: Oh... are you there together?

Martin: Hell no. We broke up. I'm on my own.

Me: Lush! How's that going? I did Bali alone a month ago and bloody loved it!

All this felt too good to be true. We'd both recently experienced long haul alone and I knew how it felt. We joked about not talking for days, dinner alone, living in hope there's wifi so that we can at least sit doing something at dinner – in his case, chatting to girls on POF.

The general chitchat, too, was perfect. I had a good feeling about this. We seemed to have a lot in common, from what we want from relationships to the kind of house we want to live in and the kind of holidays we want. It felt like I'd known him forever. He sent me daily selfies of himself, videos of him jet skiing, photos of what he was having for lunch, photos of flats he was going to view as he needed somewhere to live when he got back as he was living with the ex who wasn't on holiday with him. He even sent me a photo of his return flights information so that I could track him on his way back to the UK.

As you will have gathered by now, I am very good at stalking these boys and finding more out about them before I meet them. However, weirdly, nothing triggered in me to stalk him! What was wrong with me? The only point at which I thought, 'Oh! Why haven't I looked him up??' was when he messaged me saying he'd stalked ME on Facebook! This wasn't how it was meant to be! I'm meant to stalk! I'm the girl! Boys don't stalk! How dare he take away my joy!

Martin: I've just put your name into Facebook, and you know Julie Campbell don't you... small world, I used to go to gymnastics with her years ago!

(I don't hide my name on Whatsapp so I'm probably ever so easy to find, dammit, even though I'm a Smith!)

Me: No way... she's my cousin!

YESSSSSS, this gave me amazing stalker chances! I could just ask Julie! I obviously texted her IMMEDIATELY and asked her to tell me everything she knew about him. She didn't reply for hours. It was killing me. In the meantime I sent him the following text:

Me: If you want to fully stalk me... go ahead and add me.
Martin: That way you could stalk me back... hmm let me think about that one.

I thought he was joking but, no! He changed the subject. Odd. Alarm bells rang. Oh dear. Here we go!

Martin: How open minded are you?
Me: Thanks to online dating, I've had to become very... hit me... not literally.
Martin: In fact, remind me later, I'll tell you when you're home- and remind me later to tell you about my single life and my ex...
Me: Whaaattt such a tease!! You can't say that! It's only 12pm!

(Oh good god.)
Then nothing. Nothing at all. He didn't even come online.

This guy was having me on, wasn't he? He was playing games. And my cousin still hadn't got back to me. I was going out of my mind!

FINALLY at 6:04pm:

Martin: You home yet? xx
Me: I am!! How has the rest of your day been? Is it bedtime now in the Maldives?
Martin: Nope as I need to chat to a certain lady
Me: Any lady in particular?
Martin: Maybe...
Me: I guess it's the other POF girls then is it?
Martin: Nope, it's you... you at home and relaxed?

JESUS, JUST TELL ME!

Martin: Ok, I'm quite a deep person.
Me: Ok... good start...
Martin: What's the one thing you've always wanted?
Me: Ooooh that is a deep question!
Martin: It's not a deep question, it's a feeling from using imagination. Visualize and dream... tell me when you're done, I'll write mine and we will press send at the same time xx

How open and honest was I to be? I still didn't really know anything about this guy, yet I felt compelled to tell him things. Weird. What if he meant 'I've always wanted a dog' and I went full throttle into opening and spilling my heart out? He might run a mile. Oh well. Being honest and being me was surely the best policy, so here goes...

Me: God, hmm, ok... there are a few things that are obvious things like good health, my parents to be in good health... one day I'd love to have kids, but really all I want is someone to have by my side, who's got my back, someone to share silly stories with, to go on weekend adventures with, holidays! I'm not a materialistic person, I'm not bothered about 'things' I'm more bothered about love. There is it! That's what I've always wanted. To find love x

His response thankfully wasn't regarding wanting a dog, or a nice car:

Martin: I've always wanted someone to love me more than anything, someone to share many a memory with, someone when I come home from work to be there with open arms, a huge smile and a daughter running towards me x

Wowzers. So we kind of were on the same path. That WAS deep. Boys don't usually talk like that. Especially when we'd not even met.

Me: I'm pleased that although I went around the houses... love was also my answer

I carry on. I go for it. Why not?

Me: Have you ever been in love? Years ago I would have said I think I have... but nowadays, now I have nephews who I love so much it's ridiculous, I'm not so sure I have. And I know I've definitely never felt it off anyone. Other than off the kids. They give me pure, innocent love, it's the greatest feeling there ever was...

Martin: Thought I had been but not sure. I've also always wanted to make one particular memory where I go to a log cabin with no TV, instead a large open raging fire, being under a blanket with my gf/life partner/wife all cosy

Me: I'd actually love that. One of my dreams is to go to NYC at Christmas with a guy I love.

Martin: Maybe one day we can both experience our dreams together.

Me: Wouldn't that be great!? Soooo... what else where you going to tell me?

Martin: Just that I want to find love.

What? That was it? Really? No. No there was something else. I didn't go through all of that deepness for that to be all he had to tell me? I decided to continue to play along for the moment:

Me: Actually this reminds me to remind you to tell me about your single life. How long ago did you break up with the ex who should be there with you now? x

Martin: I was to be married the other Friday xx

What? Oh. My. God. Was he for real? I felt sick – and I wanted to laugh hysterically like a mental person.

Me: What??? OMG.

I just went with what was in my head.

Martin: This was meant to be my honeymoon x
Me: No way. Jesus. What on earth happened??
Martin: I don't know... x

This sounded complicated to me. He was meant to be married literally days ago. He was on his honeymoon on his own and now he was spilling his heart out to me, a girl he'd met on POF? He had immediately gone on POF? WAS THIS SOME KIND OF SICK JOKE? Was I being filmed for some online dating show? To prove how much girls believe? What WAS this? Surely he was in love with her if they were to get married? None of this made any sense. Jesus. Why did I open that message? Why didn't I just ignore it?

I couldn't help but ask more.

Me: Are you ok?? I'm aware I don't even know you but I feel I need to ask! Wowzers that's sad. I'm sorry to hear that. When did it all get cancelled? Who cancelled it? God I feel like I need to give you a huge hug.

It was weirdly true! I wanted to give him a hug. I had no idea what had happened; for all I knew, he could have been found cheating, he could have been seen on POF! Anything could have happened but I felt sad for him.

Martin: Can I tell you face to face?
Me: Of course... well, that's not what I expected you to say! Fair play for still going x
Martin: Which bit? x

Which bit? Was he mad? Did he think I often heard men telling me they were due to be wed on the day we started chatting?

Me: That you're actually on your honeymoon and you should be married right now... but if you were getting married... surely you were in love??

Martin: That's why I'd prefer to say in person. I can't explain over text xx

Me: Fair enough x

Martin: Still want to meet? xx

Me: For sure. Exes and pasts don't bother me... we all have them. Just got to go with the flow of life. And the flow was me deleting the evil world of online dating and your lovely little face being on that gaggle of gross... and here we are! x

Martin: Ok, shall we add each other on Facebook? This is why I didn't want to add you. Because you'll see photos of her and I together, I wanted to tell you first. Martin James.

Me: Hi Martin James. Nice to meet you xx

Martin: Added. Snoop away.

Chapter Thirty-Five

❧ ♥ ❧

So there he was. Martin James. On his honeymoon on his own. There were photos of him dining out with an old couple (like I did with Winnie and Jonnie in Bali), photos of his room, of his hotel. The works. It was actually quite sad. I obviously went back to before the honeymoon to see if I can piece any of it together. Pretty easy to work out which is his ex. She was pretty. Skinny. Blonde. There were photos of them together for at least four years, the last lot being about five months ago. That's an ok amount of time, I thought. Or is it? I have no idea!

My cousin texted back. Finally! I told her everything and asked her to tell me everything she knew. All she said was that he was lovely. Cheeky. Funny. And that she thought we'd get on. She'd not seen him for five years as she'd moved away. But from what she knew, he was nice. And engaged.

'Erm. I think he's on his honeymoon?'

I filled her in. She told me to go for it.

He waited about 20 minutes then texted me asking if I was still stalking him. I pretended I was busy changing the sheets on my bed, but of course I was still stalking him!

Me: You're ever so handsome, FYI xx

Martin: Nice flirt xx

Me: You also look ever so smiley – which is on my list of things I like in a guy x

Martin: That's me in a nut shell, happy chappy. Especially now xx

The chat continued for the rest of the time he was away. It was like having a holiday romance but not actually being there with him!

One evening I was at my sister's having dinner.

Martin: I won't bother you this evening as you mentioned you're at your sister's. I just wanted to say hi xx

Me: Hiiiii!

Martin: Haha so have you mentioned me? My ears are warm but not sure if that's sun burn xx

Me: Haha she just asked how coming off all online dating is... told her it's nice not being harassed by gross men and that a lovely one seems to have slipped into my net as I was pulling it out of the water... xx

Martin: Oh, who's that? x

Me: Just some handsome guy who annoyingly is on holiday so I have to wait to meet him. But good things come to those who wait... apparently... x

Martin: Haha when and where you meeting this guy? xx

Me: God knows... he needs to hurry home x

Martin: If I was you, I'd get him booked in soon... x

Me: So then Mr James when ARE you free?

Martin: 9th onwards, Miss Smith. Let's make a proper plan when I'm back. Why haven't I met you earlier xxxx

At the point he sent that, Michael Bublé came on the TV singing *Haven't Met You Yet*! Honestly! You couldn't make this up. I still wasn't convinced this was not part of a big TV show and Ant and Dec were about to jump out saying, 'surprise!'

The day came of his journey home. He kept me constantly updated with when he checked in, stops in airports, etc. All very exciting – and terrifying. He was my actual last hope! All the apps were gone. He wasn't meant to exist. I wasn't meant to go on any more dates with guys off apps. I was DONE!

Martin: I'm home. 23 hours later! xx
Me: Yey! Welcome! Good to have you home! x

It should have been weird saying that to someone I'd never met. But it didn't, which in itself was weird.

Martin: You talk like we've known each other for ages xx
Me: Feels like we have... or is that just me? x
Martin: I feel the same. You free on Friday night? x
Me: Sure am xx

Chapter Thirty-Six

Friday came. I got a little nervous. And I'd stopped getting nervous about dates. We chatted in the morning but neither of us mentioned the fact it was MEET day. Then it got to 5pm and I'd not heard from him for a while. This was it. This was where he bailed. Like them all. They build up hopes… only to drop you. I knew it. I was mad. I was a fool for falling for it AGAIN. I got home and decided that I'd go out and buy something nice for my tea. He wouldn't ruin my Friday night. No.

At 5:10pm my phone went.

Martin: What time and where do you want to meet? Sorry for the delay! Been stuck on a job at work xx

Oh. I unnecessarily panicked, didn't I?

Me: Is there a nice pub near you? I can drive up that way?
Martin: Do you know The Crown and Anchor? Meet there for a drink x
Me: Nope, but I have a satnav! See you at 8 xx

WHAT DO I WEAR?? I'd not done an evening date for a long time. And it was just a pub. But I had to look good. Agh. I forgot about this part of dating. Eugh. Why did I open that stupid message? Why was I doing this? I didn't want to do this any more! And here I was... doing it!

Ok, I told myself: it's easy. It's just like meeting a client from work for first time, remember. Yes. It's going to be ok.

As I got to the pub, he told me he was flashing his lights and could I see him. Yes I could. He hung up and got out of the car.

I had butterflies. He was as handsome and as smiley in real life.

'Well, hello. Nice to meet you,' he said.

'And you.'

He gave me a peck on the cheek. I almost melted. He was taller than he looked in photos. Dressed well. Smelled AMAZING. It didn't feel like I'd just met a stranger.

We went into the pub and I asked him what he wanted. I was pleased he didn't fight to be the one who bought the first drink.

'A pint of Amstel, please.'

I go crazy and order myself a pint of blackcurrant and soda water, going off course from my usual sparkling water.

We found somewhere to sit. It was a lovely cosy old pub with lots of little rooms off the main bar area. It was really busy but luckily we found a table away from anyone so that it was not obvious we were on a first date. We sat opposite each other. He sat down and just smiled at me. Didn't say anything, just sat back and smiled. It unnerved me.

'What are you smiling at?' I HAD to ask before it became super awkward as I almost didn't know where to look.

'Just you. You're even better in photos. I'm so happy I've

met you. I almost didn't. I'm still really jet lagged. But I'm glad I texted you and I'm glad I'm sitting here with you.'

We chatted about EVERYTHING. His family, my family, his job, my job. His honeymoon. My solo trip to Bali. The only thing we weren't talking about was his ex. And the marriage that didn't happen.

Finally, he said, 'Go on then... ask me.'

'Ask you what?' I replied.

He laughed. 'About my ex. I'm amazed it's not the first thing you've asked.'

So I asked away. He was the most open and honest guy I think I'd ever spoken to in my life! He did not hold back with info! Jeez! I liked it though. Very refreshing. The ex story wasn't as dramatic and interesting as I'd have hoped for. They basically fell out of love. Pretty dull really.

He told me it was obvious from my body language that I fancied him. I got embarrassed and asked what body language he was talking about.

'The way you keep playing with your hair, the way you lean towards me, the way you keep looking at me but then looking away... from where I'm sitting, I'm winning.'

I told him I have zero idea what his body language is telling me but that I guessed it was a good sign as it was almost midnight. We'd only had one drink each for four hours because we'd been non-stop chatting!

'I fancy you, Shelly. I'm so glad I found you on POF before you closed the account. We may never have met otherwise, I'm a big believer in fate and I think us meeting is fate.'

He said everything I'd wanted to hear. How did this happen? Should I have threatened to the Universe years ago that I was going to close all the dating apps down so that I'd get thrown a perfect one? Instead I'd had to kiss a few gross frogs to get here. (And get my face licked.)

He walked me to my car – where we found a homeless man sitting next to it. Awks. I said 'That's me', slightly embarrassed at battered old Bridgette, my Clio.

I got that usual fear of what to do when we say bye. A kiss? Peck on cheek? Peck on lips? Just a hug? Just say bye? I wasn't even drunk!

He said, ever so quietly, 'It's been very lovely to meet you, Miss Smith. I do hope we can do this again soon. Please text me when you get home so I know you're safe.'

He bent down and gave a gentle peck on the lips. Fireworks nearly went off in my stomach. All I could say back was, 'you too'. I then giggled awkwardly and got in my car.

Once home, I texted him as requested.

Me: Hello lovely Martin James. I am home. Thanks for a very lovely evening. xx

Martin: Thanks for letting me know you're home safely. I really enjoyed tonight, had such a nice time. Oh and you have nice soft lips, might have wanted to kiss you more but there was a guy directly behind us so a peck was just enough xx

Me: Haha I know! Snap ;) I think he stopped there on purpose. You really are ever so lovely. Let me know when you'd like to do it again xx

Martin: When are you next free? xx

Me: Forever. I'm free every night till you move in ha-haha ;)

Martin: I'd like to see you again very soon. Hope you're smiling right now xx

Me: ☺ xxxx

I woke up in the morning to a text:

Martin: Morning, how you doing? Do anything good last night? I met a special lady xx

Me: Morning! Ooh sounds exciting! Weirdly... I met a lovely guy... x

Martin: Oh my days we are both lucky then. But did you get a cheeky lips kiss? xx

Me: I did! But a pervy man decided to sit behind and watch! xx

Martin: Really?? That happened to me!! x

Me: Shut the front door?? x

Martin: Was yours handsome? My lady was beautiful. x

Me: He was EVER so handsome x

Martin: I'm hopefully going to meet her again soon x

Me: Me too! Fingers crossed! x

Martin: Are you free on Wednesday, Miss Smith? x

Me: I am xx

We chatted more over the weekend. He was actually lovely! Who knew?! We planned to meet in the Trafford Centre on Wednesday evening.

I must not get excited. This was always my problem. I get giddy and it all goes wrong! No. Must. Stay. Neutral.

Me: Morning!! Happy WEDNESDAY!! xx

Martin: Is it WEDNESDAY already??? xx

Me: It IS! xx

Martin: Looking forward to seeing you later... a little bit... I don't want to sound too keen xx

Me: Looking forward to seeing you too. Meet you in Costa at 6pm xx

There he was, standing in Costa. Looking just as handsome as before. I don't know why I'd expected him to look any different!

He gave me a peck on the cheek and smelled as divine as last time. It felt like we were a couple who had been together for years. We sat down and chatted and drank our coffees. He then suggested we go to Nando's as he'd never been! What man has never been to Nando's? This is madness!

I taught him how it works. He seemed very confused by the concept but went with it. (And ordered mash. Who orders mash in Nando's?)

He told me that he felt I kept my cards very close to my chest on date one and although my body language suggested I was interested, I wasn't giving much away. He asked about my relationship history. As I questioned him on Friday, I thought it was only fair I was open and honest in return. I told him pretty much everything about the significant few. He was shocked by the crazy fireman and couldn't believe what I was telling him was true. I told him this is why I struggled with guys who I met online: I found it hard to trust them and it took me a while to believe and trust everything they were saying so he may have to bear with me. He was very understanding.

We were going to go to the cinema but a) I'm not a huge cinema fan and b) I don't think it's such a good idea on a date as you can't talk. We seemed to enjoy talking so instead we went to a bar for a drink. I was growing to like him more and more by the second. It was ridiculous. We played the game of trying to work out who in there was on a date, what number date it was, who was married, who was happy in the relationship, etc.

He stopped and looked at me and said, 'If anyone else in here is playing this game – which they probably aren't because

they aren't kids like us – I think they'd think we've been together for years. And I like that thought.'

Oh come on now! Stop saying these perfect things. You
cannot be real.

Once again we chatted nonsense for so long that the bar
was closing and we had to leave. He walked me to my car
again where this time a large family were fighting, trying to get
the kids into the car next to me.

He said, 'Sod this, not again,' and properly kissed me.
I stopped noticing the arguing family, because this handsome
man was smooching me and I didn't care who saw. I wanted
him to get in my car and come home with me. But no. That's
not how this works. Instead he gave me one final kiss and said,
'Text me when you're home'.

Me: I'm home. Thank you for another lovely night xxx
Martin: You're welcome for tonight. Another success-
ful date. We are getting good at this dating malarkey.
And oh my... what a kiss xx
Me: We've been together for years! Of course we are
good are this dating malarkey x
Martin: Feel like I've known you for years in a great
way xx
Me: Snap. Weird huh. Night. Have a happy sleep xx

The following day I was heading off to London for work so
I was up early to catch an early train. I noticed I already had
a text:

Martin: Sooo am I reading the signals properly... Are
we keen on each other xx

I couldn't decide if that was a weird text. He's a boy, I reasoned. And boys are weird. And so far he'd not been a normal boy: he seemed to have the ability to show his emotions.

I didn't really know what to reply. How did I know if he was keen on me? And keen? What a rubbish word!

Me: If you are keen on me, then you are correct, I am keen on you x

Was that the worst response I'd ever given? Bloody keen. He just replied with: 'Good good ☺'.
Followed by:

Martin: Best way is to be open and honest. I've been honest and open with from the start and I intend on remaining that way... I really enjoy your company, you're funny easy to talk to, intelligent, good morals and attractive exactly what I'm looking for in a partner and partner in crime lol xxx xx
Me: Snap.
Martin: Sooo let's keep smiling and continue on this road to potential happiness xxx

Chapter Thirty-Seven

---💛💛— ♥ —💛💛---

So I guessed he really was 'keen'. Guys were never this 'keen'. It unnerved me. I shouldn't be unnerved, should I? I should just enjoy it for once. Take the compliments? I find taking compliments hard as I'm not used to them at all. I would just go with the flow. I spent the rest of the train journey re-reading that conversation trying to work out if it really happened. It's normally us girls who overthink stuff! Not the guys. I then opened Facebook and tried to work him out some more. There were photos of him and his ex. This was normal. She looked normal. She looked happy. He looked happy. I wonder what REALLY happened. Did they really just fall out of love? I tried not to spend the day thinking about it, and thinking about him. I needed to concentrate on this meeting in London!

My train home was at 7pm. I messaged him when on the train asking how his day had been. He'd spent most of it on Rightmove trying to find a flat to live in.

Me: What shall we do on date three? Something fun & random? x
Martin: GoApe? xx

It was at this point I remembered I'm like a broken old lady. I got carried away in yoga and doing weights in the gym and basically screwed my shoulder up. I never learn...

Me: Sounds ace!! Although... will it be bad for my stupid shoulder? x
Martin: Ah maybe... hmm... don't want you hurt... you're PC xx
Me: PC? x
Martin: Precious Cargo xxx

That was one of the nicest things anyone had ever called me. Genuinely! I must not cry on the train. I must not cry on the train.

I just reply with: 'Love that xx'.

Martin: I really like your smile. I really like the taste of your lips. And as long as you don't think I'm being too forward and don't mind me saying this but in the distant future (no rush whatsoever on this) but I look forward to making love to you xx

Then moments later:

Martin: Oh dear not sure I should of said that...
Me: Ha I've told you, you can say what you like. I generally like what you say... I'm not used to guys saying nice stuff to me, so it's nice to actually hear for once in my life! Which is probably why I'm not good at taking a compliment as I don't know what you do with them! xx
Martin: When shall we go on date three then? Sunday? x

It was now Thursday so Sunday sounded good.

Me: I'm at a christening in the morning but YES after that? xx

Martin: Perfect. I shall look forward. I'm off to bed now. Sweet dreams, smiler xx

The next day, something weird happened. We only exchanged five messages all day. Now, I'm aware in some people's lives exchanging two messages with someone you've only been on two dates with is a lot, but he was a texter. A deep heavy texter...

I tried to make conversation, asking questions about the flats he'd viewed. He replied three hours later:

Martin: Sorry just got out of the gym. Viewings went really well thanks just one more on sat then I decide xx

I decided to be normal. We had only had two dates. He didn't HAVE to text me...

Me: Like the ones you've seen then? x

Nothing. No reply. I sent it at 15:59. He didn't come back online AT ALL, ALL DAY. (I obviously kept obsessively checking his last seen on Whatsapp time.)

I woke up in the morning at 7am and checked. Still no reply. And he was last online at 2am? WTF? What on earth had happened? Was he ok? This was SO odd. Or was it? I didn't actually know him. I didn't know his actual life pattern. I could tell you his life pattern from when he was in the Maldives but I didn't know real life patterns.

I decided again to be normal. I sent him a message.

Me: Morning! Happy Friday! xxxx

NOTHING. NOTHING AT ALL. He did come online at some point and did read my message but didn't reply. WHAAATTT? How could someone go from 'I can't wait to make love to you' to NOTHING? Made. Zero. Sense.

Had he actually been playing me all this time? Was he dating loads of girls? Saying the same romantic stuff to them? Were we all falling for it? I didn't know what to do. I felt sick. I was annoyed. Gutted. Outraged. What should I do? Nothing? Just add him to my LONG list of 'and then he disappeared'? NO! I was not having it! People don't say the stuff he said to then disappear. This was NOT ok. I WAS COMING OFF ONLINE DATING TO AVOID THIS!

15:03:

Martin: Hiya just finished work how's your day. x

What? He surely can't not reply for 24 hours, to then just say that? With zero explanation? Was I being mental? Had I turned into a psycho? Had online dating finally turned me into one of 'them'? He didn't even respond to my question from 24 hours before! What do I reply? I wanted to write all of this to him. I turned to my friends for assistance. I decided I could no longer be in control of this. I had no idea what to say.

They told me to just play it cool. Be normal. See what happened. But to not ask a question.

Me: Good thanks. Usual busy Friday. x

Three hours later he replied:

Martin: What a day. Hope yours has been ok x
Me: I'd rather be in Bali! You had a tough one? x

DAMN it! I asked a question! AGH!
He didn't respond. So the next day I simply texted:

Me: Morning. Is everything ok? x

He responded instantly.

Martin: Morning sorry... been mad busy with work
etc. little stressed finding a place to live.

With no kisses. Nothing. I was gutted. Empty almost. I decided not to reply. If he was interested, he'd text again.

He was just like all the others, wasn't he. I thought he was my fate. My sliding door. How can guys do this to girls? Pick you up, put you so high. And drop you. BOOM.

The following day was the Christening of Lucy's baby. The day we were meant to be going on a date. I spent all of the Christening trying not to look at my phone to see if he'd sent a text. Maybe he WAS really stressed with flat hunting and he'd text with an amazing date idea and sweep me off my feet. Yes. Let's not give up just yet! There may have been a reason. A good reason. But no. I waited until 3pm after the Christening and I send him the following:

Me: Hey, so I feel like it'd be weird if I said nothing...
and you're all about being open & honest, so here
goes... What has happened between Thursday evening

& Friday? You went from being excited about a future with me to practically nothing. As you said you don't want to waste my time & vice versa. So if you can please just be honest & tell me what has happened, I'd massively appreciate it. I'm also presuming date three today is no longer happening... x

I sat and waited. I took off my make up. My dress. Took out my contact lenses. Put on my joggers and my hoodie and waited. Nothing. I couldn't believe it. Genuinely could not believe it. Another one had done it. Was it me? Was I doing something wrong? I MUST be! They all did the same. It made no sense. What was going on?

The following morning I got up early, dragged my sorry ass out of bed and went spinning. I needed to sweat this out. I needed to do something to feel good about myself. Little Mix *Shout Out To My Ex* was the first song in the class. I wanted to sing along to it out loud in a rage but I was aware I really would look like one of those psycho girls. So I quietly 'span' my legs as fast and as hard as I could.

I came out to discover a message from him.

Martin: Hi Shelly sorry been busy stressed and anxious recently. Got a lot on my plate at the minute with family and life in general, everything is getting a little on top of me and I'm beginning to crack. I've got to find my own place as that's my main priority along side my business. I'm sorry if you feel I've been distant... I think it's probably best that I sort myself out before anything else as it's not fair on you to keep you in the dark. Sorry Shelly you're a lovely woman and I hate messing people around. If I can keep your

number and if you're still single we can meet up again
in the future if not I understand x

Wow, there it was. These men will forever blow my mind. (I was also amused he called me a woman. I don't think I've ever been referred to as a woman.) I didn't know if I believed him or not. But to be honest, I'd prefer to think that is what happened rather than anything else and at least he did reply.

So there he went. My one last online date. Gone. Just like that.

Chapter Thirty-Eight

Back to life. To reality. In a world where I wasn't an online dater. It felt weird out here – actually quite nice and simple and peaceful. I had a lot more time on my hands. I could watch TV programmes without disruption from my phone pinging saying, 'Congratulations! You have got a new match!' or 'JonnyBeGood has sent you a message'. I went out for dinner with friends where I had other things to talk about rather than my most recent online dating disaster. I wasn't constantly worrying that I accidentally may have swiped left on the man of my dreams and he may now be gone forever. One of the main bonuses was that my phone battery lasted so much longer!

Christmas came and went. Yet another one on my own. But, actually, it was ok. I bought myself a gift up to the value of what I'd spend on a boyfriend had I had one – a Garmin watch and some new trainers as I was going to have even more time to spend exercising – and I was able to do whatever I wanted with whoever I wanted across the festive period. Free to go wherever I wanted. Until I got flu. And I became a prisoner in my own home. Having to get myself glasses of water mid coughing fit. Having to grate my own ginger into cups of hot water with tea and lemon. I only had Phillip Schofield for company for the first few days of 2017. But then, after day seven of flu on my own, I had a moment.

I suddenly appreciated all the things I was surrounded by. The super comfy sofa was my choice, the pictures on the walls were mine, all the candles I had lit were lovely. Everything in my lounge was so nice and cosy. And I'd made it that way all on my own. I realised I didn't want someone to nurse me, I was getting better on my own in my own way. Many of my friends and family are in relationships where they're not particularly happy, and I realised how happy I was. Happy just being me. With zero complications. In my simple, easy, quiet life. On my sofa, under a blanket, drinking tea and eating a Mars Bar.

I decided being single really wasn't so bad.

For starters, I can starfish in bed and sleep in peace with no snoring next to me or no one stealing the duvet. If my flat is cold, I don't have to 'put more layers on', I can turn up the heating as much as I like. Not having to keep my legs shaved is a massive bonus of being single and I don't have to do anyone else's washing other than my own and if I want to leave my washing up on the side for days... I can! Weekends are free to do whatever I want and with whoever I want. I don't have to go and see the in-laws on a Sunday, and I don't have to have forced friendships with my other half's mates' other halves! I have time to spend seeing my friends without worrying about splitting my time or being accused of 'binning off my mates for a boy'. I don't have to leave a party because my boyfriend is too drunk. And I don't risk being sick on or peed on by my boyfriend when he's too drunk and thinks the bathroom is where my bedside table is. I don't have to watch boy stuff on TV, and I can watch *Eat Pray Love* as many times as I like. I don't need to leave space in the fridge for beers; I can fill it lovingly with tonic for my gin and as much smelly cheese as I like. I can have whatever I fancy for dinner, even if it's a bowl of cereal or a large bar of chocolate. And I can't be judged for eating nothing but a large bar of chocolate as no one but me knows I've done it. If I'm not in the mood to chat, I can sit happily in silence without being questioned if I'm ok. And I can hang as many wooden hearts around my flat as I like without anyone rolling their eyes at me when I make yet another wooden heart purchase. I don't have to constantly question if I'm 'just settling' and I don't have the constant worry of being let down or being disappointed. I can go on holiday to wherever I want and whenever I want and can spend as much money – or as little money – in doing so as I want. Being single is pretty damn amazing!

People feel sorry for me and ask why I'm single. They presume I'm lonely – but I'm really not. I'm having the best time filling my days with fun and I really do love my life and I feel lucky to be single- that said, I would gladly make room for the right man should I bump into him anytime soon.

Maybe everyone was right. Once I stopped looking, he would appear. GO UNIVERSE! DO WHAT YOU NEED TO DO! BRING ME MY MAN! I PROMISE I'LL STOP OBSESSIVELY LOOKING FOR HIM ON THE INTERNET. Until then, I shall continue to enjoy living this uncomplicated, happy single life.

8th January 2017, 4am. A text. From Paris Pete.

Hey trouble... how you doing? x

Oh god. Here we go again.

The End

Acknowledgements

There are many people I'd like to thank but it'd be impossible to name them all as I have so many wonderful friends and family who have supported me not just throughout the writing of this book but also through the tough times and the happy times ☺.

Firstly thanks to Lisa for suggesting I do this in the first place.

Thanks to Sarah and Amy for reading this for me before I decided to do anything with it – and putting my paranoia to bed. To Beth for not only reading it but also helping to proof read it – legend.

To my other sisters Linda and Rach – thanks for being constantly available on Whatsapp when I've been heart broken. To Michelle, Faye, Sally, Anna, James, Shelley, Laura and Azza for the use of your ears and wine over the years. To Emma for all of your help and blackcurrant and sodas. To Nat and Sam for staying forever on the single shelf with me. And to both sets of parents for being truly amazing and making me the person I am today – I'd be lost without you all.

I'd like to thank Tinder, Plenty of Fish, Bumble, eHarmony, Match.com, OkCupid, Happn and Zoosk for opening up this absolutely crazy world of online dating to me.

And finally, I'd like to thank all the guys that I've met – whether you've messed me about or not… without you, this book would not exist.

Lightning Source UK Ltd.
Milton Keynes UK
UKOW04f1954281117
313528UK00001B/301/P